From: yh

VICKY:
THE FLOWER GIRL

AIMEE-LYNN JOHNSON

Copyright © 2015 by Aimee-Lynn Johnson

Vicky: The Flower Girl
by Aimee-Lynn Johnson

Printed in the United States of America

ISBN 9781498423311

Scripture quotations are taken from the New International Version (NIV). Copyright © 1973, 1978, 1984, 2011 by Biblica, Inc.™. Used by permission. All rights reserved.

Scripture quotations taken from the New King James Version (NKJV). Copyright © 1979, 1980, 1982 by Thomas Nelson, Inc. Used by permission. All rights reserved.

www.xulonpress.com

To McKenna,
Don't ever stop writing.

I am extending thanks to the following people: mom, dad, Jeff, Melva Roley, Brian Clark, Rachel Smith, Bob Carstenson, and Katie Hoover, for the editing help, time-off, advice, prayer and/or support. Thank you Cari Caryl and Jose Medina for helping me make my dream come true. Thank you to my church family for the support as well. Here's a big thank you to my Curves family for letting me talk about my book.

Lastly, God, thank you for giving me a story to share. Thank you for being there for me, and encouraging me to go on even when I wanted to quit and give up.

1

VICKY

"God, I need you every hour of every day. I need you and I long for you. I have gotten so far from you, and I don't know the way back. Please, lead me and bring me back to you. I don't know how I got here; please don't let me stay here. I'm done living a life that doesn't have passion. I'm tired of the emptiness. Please save me from this road I'm on. It's not just about doing something that makes me happy, I want to put my whole self in; my whole heart, my soul, my everything; into my life. It's about waking up in the morning and saying, 'Wow, it's good to be alive.' God, I want to be completely sold out to your son, Jesus. God, you know my heart, you know what I need, you know what I want, and you know everything even before I ask. I am asking you here in this moment, to reignite my passion for you. Thank you for your blessings in my life. Thank you for my car, this apartment that I am sitting in at this moment, and yes, even my job. Thank you for all you've given me. Please help me to find the path that leads toward you."

Filling the air with thanksgiving made her feel better.

She sat on her bed, with her head bowed and her eyes closed.

Cara opened her eyes, and looked up at the ceiling, and then she said, "Thank you for never giving up on me."

Her cheeks were wet from crying, and her eyes burned. Cara wiped her tears away, and blew her nose into a Kleenex from the box on her dresser. Some tears had landed on her forearms, so she grabbed a fresh tissue to dry them. Her sobbing had been quiet, but her emotions behind the tears were not. She felt empty. She had felt that way for several months, but it wasn't until that moment that she really felt ready to change. Before she had wanted to change the way her life was headed, but she hadn't been ready.

What made the difference? Why that moment? Her brother and his wife had just had their second child, and they were a family. It made her realize just how lonely she felt. She lived by herself, and had her own life. She had sought after independence, and that's how she lived her life.

"God, I feel so lost," she said, another tear sliding down, she shook her head, "but fear surrounds me. I am afraid of falling, that I won't be able to get back up. I am afraid that if I leave my job, I won't be able to find more. I can't go anywhere. I feel so...stuck. Where did I go wrong?"

Cara was tired and had an overwhelming desire to have God as the head of her life once again. She grabbed another tissue, and wiped the tear. As she did this she smiled a little, saying, "Thank you, God, that I haven't put on mascara, yet," and she laughed a little.

The laughter made her feel good to some extent, but she still longed for the piece that was missing from her life. If you could have recorded her life on an EKG, you would see rhythm like a comatose patient: alive but not really living. She was living by herself and for herself.

You might want to get dressed, she heard the quiet voice in her mind say.

She slid off her bed onto the short-fiber carpeting. She slid the door of her closet open, and she looked at the assortment of shirts, skirts, shoes, and other accessories. Everything had a place, and you could navigate through it easily. It was just like the rest of her life: a neat order that was manageable. There was nothing wrong with being organized, but her day-to-day routine was starting to wear on her.

Her closet illustrated how she was living by herself; everything in it belonged to her. In that moment she wanted nothing more than to live for someone else and to share her life and all the blessings that God had given her. She thought about her brother, who was sharing his life with those he loved.

She pulled a sky blue, short-sleeve, button-up blouse and a pair of light-grey shorts. As she put them on, she thought about being a mom someday. Maybe when her daughter was old enough, she would steal Cara's clothes. She laughed a little at that. In that time of someday she would be married and living in a house, perhaps with a Labrador retriever that would greet her when she got home, barking excitedly. She could just imagine a big yellow lab, which would be just as much a part of the family as any of the people. There would be a fence around the yard, and kids' toys throughout the house and all over the yard. In her imagination she could see her brother and his wife bringing their kids over to her house for family gatherings like Thanksgiving and Christmas, and Jeff's children would play with Cara's children, just like Jeff and Cara played together when they were little. There would be quite an age gap between them, but they would get along just fine. Uncle Jeff and Aunt Allison, the titles fit very well. Jeff was showing himself to be a very devoted and loving father; she could only imagine what he'd be like with Cara's children. Imagining having a family just made Cara want to have one of her own all the more.

A family, that's what Cara wanted most in the world. Not only a chance to be a wife, but to be a mother. Further into the future, she would be a grandmother. It was all so wonderful to imagine. Even a temporary guardianship wouldn't be that bad, she figured.

She started to thank God for the little things like her life, her health, her job, her car, her independence. At first, it was a struggle to name things she was thankful for, but as the list grew, it became easier and her mood lifted. She thanked God for that victory.

In the next moment, she heard footsteps on the stairs to her apartment. The cement stairwell echoed whenever anyone stepped onto them, even if they tried to not make a sound. The person coming up the stairs was running fast, and they sounded much too light to be an adult, no, it sounded more like a child.

Cara expected the person to stop at an apartment on the second floor, but they were coming closer to the third floor. In Cara's section of the apartment complex, there were only two occupants on the third floor, Cara and an elderly woman who lived across from her and didn't have any visitors. Before the footsteps stopped, Cara moved from her bedroom through the living area to the door. Then the footsteps stopped, and there were three fast knocks on her door, and then she heard a young voice say through the door, "Can you help me, please?"

Let her in, Cara heard the quiet voice say.

Cara had the door open, before anything else could be said. Her eyes fell to the girl standing on the doorstep. Cara was alarmed to see such a young girl on her doorstep so early in the morning. The girl seemed frightened and about ready to cry. Immediately upon seeing the girl, Cara told her to come into her apartment.

After the girl was inside and the door was closed and latched, Cara turned to the girl, "What's happened?" she asked.

"I've become separated from my parents, and some bad men are after me."

"How?"

"We were at the gas station near your house, and my mom and I went into the store and...and bad guys-the men who are after me-came into the store. My mom told me to hide, so I did. She said I couldn't let those men find me or see me, because if they did, it would have been very bad."

"Who are they and why do they want you?" Cara urged gently.

"Bad men who want to use me to..."

"To what? What do they want to use you for? What do they want you to do?"

The little girl bit her lower lip, "Can you keep a secret?" she whispered.

"Yes, what is it?"

The girl indicated for Cara to come closer to her level. Cara moved closer to the girl. The girl leaned in to whisper in Cara's ear, but then she moved away from Cara's ear, and said, "Wait, can I have your name first?"

"My name? Why?"

"Because, I can't tell a stranger my secret."

"OK, my name is Cara Stenfeld. What's yours'?"

"Victoria Fields, but I go by 'Vicky', only my daddy calls me 'Victoria'."

"So what is the secret, Vicky?" Cara whispered.

The little girl, Vicky leaned in close to Cara, she cupped her hands around her mouth, as she whispered, "I can turn into a plant," into Cara's ear.

Cara backed up a little bit, "What?" she demanded.

Vicky indicated Cara to come closer, and then she whispered, "I can turn into a plant," again.

Cara said, "I heard you the first time, but I'm confused. How do you turn into a plant?"

"May I show you?" Vicky asked.

"I guess so."

"Do you have a large pot?"

"A what?"

"A large pot."

"I should have one." Cara stood up and walked over to the coat closet.

Cara dug through her closet, until she came up with a black plastic flower pot about two feet tall and about a foot and a half in diameter.

"Will this work?" she asked, holding it up for Vicky to see.

"That's perfect," Vicky informed her. "Do you have any soil?"

"Soil, yeah."

Cara set the pot down in the kitchen, and pulled a small bag of potting soil out from under the sink. She said to Vicky standing in the living room, "There isn't a lot, here. I've been using it mostly for small plants."

Vicky came into the kitchen, "That'll work," she said.

"Are you sure?"

"Yep, dump it in."

Cara dumped the rest of the bag into the flower pot, it was just enough to cover the bottom about an inch.

Vicky stepped into the pot, and then she said, "Cara, watch this."

Cara watched as there was a little girl standing in the pot one second, and a flowering tree in the next instant. She gasped, "Oh my," she said.

There was a little girl standing there once again.

"That's how I can turn into a plant."

"You certainly do."

Vicky looked up at Cara with big, green eyes that were such a bright, vivid green they reminded Cara of grass on a spring day. Then Vicky asked, "So, what'd you think?"

Cara stuttered a moment trying to find the right words to say, it was the most unusual thing she'd ever experienced, but how could she convey that without hurting the girl's feelings? She was amazed, but she was also very unsure what to feel.

Finally Cara said, "That has got to be the most amazing thing I have ever seen."

Vicky replied, "Do you want to see me do something else?"

"No, thank you," Cara said.

"The bad guys want you for that?" Cara asked.

"Well, it's a grown-up thing I don't get at all."

"A grown-up thing?"

"My parents call it a colored letter. They say it's a bad thing."

"Colored letter?"

"Yeah, like blue or grey. Only, it's not either of those colors, it's black. They call it 'blackmail'."

"Blackmail? The bad guys want to use you to blackmail? Who, your parents?"

"No, not my parents. Other people with jobs. What does blackmail mean anyways?"

"It means to hold something over someone's head, in order to man...make someone do what you want them to do."

"*Oh*, that's not very nice. Does listening in on conversations count as blackmail?"

"Yes. You can listen in on conversations?"

"Yep, like when I turned into a tree for you just now, I heard you," she inhaled sharply, then she said in a voice trying to mimic Cara's," 'Oh my!' "

"You could hear me?"

"Of course."

"That means that...in an office you could...in a top security place...in the stock exchange."

Cara was going through in her mind everywhere Vicky could go to listen in on potentially sensitive information. If she could understand everything that was said, then that meant that she could be really dangerous in the wrong hands.

Cara then asked, "Can you make out everything you hear? I mean, as a plant, can you hear things as clearly as you can hear them right now, as you are talking to me?"

"Yeah. Actually I can hear better, somehow."

"You can hear things better as a plant."

"Yeah."

"That's why your mom said if they saw you or found you, it would be bad. She told you to hide, to protect you."

Vicky agreed, "Yeah. She told me when they were gone, to run to safety, and she would come back for me."

"Why did you come to me?" Cara wondered.

Vicky shrugged, "God led me to you."

"God, led you to me?"

She nodded her head, "Well, after I escaped from the gas station I started running across the street to your... your neighborhood?"

"Apartment complex."

"Apartment complex. Anyways, God told me where to go. He said that I was to run to the top of a certain flight of stairs, knock on the door on the left, and who-ever lived there would let me in, and know how to pro-tect me. He also told me that the person 'is ready to have their heart opened to love.' "

"He said that?"

"Yep, and that I was to ask you, if you would please protect me with all you've got, even if that means that you lose."

"Lose what?"

"What matters most to you?"

21

"What matters most to me?"

"But in exchange for helping me, you will be rewarded."

"How?"

Vicky smiled a little bit, "I don't know." Then Vicky said more seriously, "Cara will you please protect me?"

Cara knew it would not be easy, the potential for loss was very great, and if the men found out Vicky was staying at Cara's apartment, it would be very bad; but beyond all these things Cara knew that if she didn't protect this young girl, she would regret it for the rest of her life. The little girl was far more important than what she could lose or gain or her own safety. To return Vicky to her parents unharmed would be the best thing she could do. She didn't know what the reward looked like, only that there would be one, whatever it was. In her heart, she hoped it meant that her life would no longer be like a car idling, but the light would turn green, and she would be able to move forward in her life.

To Vicky she said, "Yes, I will protect you. With everything I've got and to the best of my abilities."

2

LILY

Fifteen Minutes Earlier...

Douglas Fields gripped the steering wheel, and looked out at the road disappearing beneath his car. He blinked his eyes, and shook his head. He blinked his eyes a second time. It was five thirty in the morning, and there wasn't much traffic.

The road ahead was very mesmerizing. He shook his head again. Douglas had to stay awake; his family was depending on him. His three children and his wife Lily were in the car with him. Lily turned into a human, and she immediately asked, "Are you ready for me to drive?"

He nodded his head. He had driven all night and into the early morning, and he was more than ready for Lily to take her stretch of the trip. When she grew tired and was ready for him to take over once more, he would. That's how they travelled on long trips, he usually started out, then she would take over, then he would take over, then she would take over. That way, they could get to their destination as quickly as possible.

On that particular trip, they were driving up from their home in Southern California to Washington to visit Lily's father. The family made the trek once a year.

Douglas looked at the fuel gauge; the needle was touching the top of the E.

"I'm going to find a gas station, and we'll switch, okay?" he explained.

"Yeah," she replied.

He took an exit off the freeway.

"Where are we?" she asked.

"We are half an hour away from Portland."

"We are?"

"Yep."

"All right."

He turned onto a main street, and into a gas station with a convenience store.

An attendant ran to them, "Fill it up, regular," Douglas said before the young man could ask.

"Will you be paying cash or charge?" he asked.

Lily answered, "I'll pay cash, inside."

"You got it."

The attendant grabbed the nozzle and inserted it into the gas tank.

She unbuckled her seatbelt, and to her husband she said, "I'll get some bottles of water."

She leaned over to him and gave him a quick kiss.

"Hurry up," he told her.

Then they heard from the backseat, "Can I come, too?"

They both turned to see Vicky, their youngest, standing there. Vicky rubbed her eye with one hand. Douglas and Lily exchanged a glance.

"Go," Douglas told Vicky, his daughter.

Lily waited for the attendant to give them the receipt, and then she and Vicky got out of the car. Lily grabbed Vicky's small hand, and held it as they walked across the pavement into the store.

"We have to do this quickly," Lily informed her. She grabbed a basket and gave it to Vicky.

"There are five people in our family, and I want to get four bottles of water per person. How many total water bottles do I need?"

"Twenty," Vicky replied.

"Good job," she said, leading her over to the beverage cooler; all the while she watched the other people in the store. There was a man with a grey mustache wearing a light brown leather vest, purchasing cigarettes; a man (much younger) in work overalls buying coffee; and two women at the cashier counter: one woman had short, blond hair tied back with a navy scrunchee, and the other woman was older with long, dark hair.

At the cooler, Lily and Vicky started grabbing water bottles and putting them into the basket, when all of a sudden Lily's phone vibrated. She dropped the two water bottles she had grabbed, and pulled the phone out of her pocket to see a text from her husband. When she opened the message, she saw the words, "Code Red", which, in the color-code system she and her husband had developed meant danger with possible imminent threat to persons.

Lily immediately snapped into mama bear mode, and she tried to figure a way to protect Vicky.

"Vicky," she said, "I need you to find a place to hide."

"Where?"

Lily saw two doors leading to a back storeroom, "Behind those doors, in that area. Then you need to get out of here."

Vicky looked at the doors.

"Go!" she urged, and then she said, "We'll come back for you when it's safe."

Vicky stumbled behind the doors and into a corner, where she would not be seen. No sooner had she disappeared then two men came into the store.

Immediately Lily saw that one of them had a tattoo of rose thorns and leaves circling his upper arm. They were the type of men who wanted to use children like Vicky to listen in on conversations.

Lily was careful to look away from the door that was still swinging as she walked up to the cashier with the short, blond hair because she was closer to the door. She started scanning the water bottles. As much as she could, Lily tried to keep an eye on the two men.

"Is that it for you?" she asked.

"Uh, this, too," Lily said, handing her the receipt. The cashier tapped some buttons on the screen in front of her.

"Your total comes to $173.75. Is that all?" the cashier asked.

"Yes."

"Would you like to pay cash or charge?"

"Cash," Lily said, pulling two hundred dollars from her wallet.

The cashier entered the amount, and then said, "Your change is $26.25." She pulled the amount from the till.

After she had counted back the change, she happened to look up into Lily's eyes. The best way to identify a potted person is the unusual vividness of their eyes.

"Your eyes are amazing," the cashier said.

"Thanks," Lily mumbled, grabbing the bags of water bottles, and trying to get out as fast as she could.

Then she heard, "Didn't you have a young girl with you?"

"No."

"About six?"

"No," Lily replied sharply. She could feel the interest of everyone in the store. Even the two men were interested. She walked on outside. At the car, she got in the passenger seat in the front, dropping the bags on the floor of the backseat.

Her husband, upon seeing her so distraught said, "Perhaps I should drive?"

"Just go!" she insisted.

He pulled away from the gas station.

"Where's Vicky?" he demanded.

"I'll tell you, but first, we need to get out of here. Find somewhere we can pray," she said.

He sighed, "Let me find a parking lot, so we may pray."

He found a parking lot about a half mile away for a small coffee shop, and he pulled into a parking space.

"Where's Vicky?" he inquired once more but gentler this time.

Lily poured out her heart, and told him everything that had happened, "We were in the store grabbing water bottles, when I received your text. I told Vicky to find somewhere to hide, and to get out. Then I told her, I would come back for her when it was safe to do so. Then the men came into the store, and one cashier commented about my eyes and the other saw Vicky with me and was starting to ask me about her. So I panicked, and I left her. I felt if I went back, they would surely find her. So I did what I had to do. That's why we need to pray for her. Do you think I did the right thing?"

"I think you said correctly when you said you did what you had to do."

"I didn't want to have to fight with those men. I imagine if they had seen Vicky, it could have been a struggle. I didn't think I could take on two men by myself, at least not without using my abilities; which would have revealed it to everyone in the store."

"Lily," Douglas said gently, "it's time to pray. That's all we can do for Vicky right now. Sarah, John, please come here," he said to two small plants in the very back seat.

Immediately there were two children coming closer.

"We need to pray," Douglas said. "Will you two join us?"

Sarah nodded her head, "We will," she said.

The parents sat in the front seats, and Sarah and John sat in the seats right behind them. The family grabbed each others' hands, bowed their heads and closed their eyes.

Then Lily began to pray, "Heavenly Father, we need you to protect our little Vicky. Don't let those men find her. Lead her to someone who will keep her safe. Perhaps, God, someone who is up for a new challenge and who won't use Vicky's abilities for any personal gain. I am asking for a woman who will love Vicky as her own daughter..."

Next Douglas added, "I agree with my wife, Father God, but I want to add that the woman knows you, and not only that, but desires you above all else. You would give her wisdom to lead, and she would depend solely on you, God."

John put in, "Please, bring my sister safely back to us."

Lastly Sarah said, "In Jesus' name we pray..."

Everyone said, "Amen!" and they all opened their eyes. Lily looked around at her family, and she was utterly amazed by them. Douglas, her husband, had such a dependency on God that he was always willing to jump in and pray. Sarah, her nine year old, and John, her seven year old, were growing as individuals with hearts for God. It was amazing to see. Everyone was tired, but they were all willing to pray for Vicky's safety. It warmed her heart.

Thank you, Father, she said silently, *for giving me a family that is sensitive to you.*

Out loud she said, "Thank you everybody, so much."

She could feel God's presence in the car, and she was filled with a calm confidence of knowing God had everything under control. As much as Lily loved her daughter, she knew it could never measure up to how much God loved her and her daughter. It meant that in the long run, things would be okay, but it would be bumpy in the short-term.

God had a person in mind to protect Vicky, and the person was Cara Stenfeld. Cara was in a unique position to protect Vicky, and she would do so with her whole heart.

3

THE RHODODENDRON GARDEN

Cara and Vicky were walking down the stairs to Cara's car waiting down below. They had decided to go to the Crystal Springs Rhododendron Garden, to see if they could find Vicky's parents. Vicky had asked about a garden, and Cara had gone there many times on her days off to be by herself. It was a big garden with many varieties of rhododendrons. The garden would be a good place for someone with the ability to turn into a plant to hideout at.

Cara had built-in car seats in her car, and they were perfect for Vicky.

They were on the road soon after.

As soon as they were on the road, Cara called her boss to let him know that she wouldn't be in to work that day. While she was talking, she heard the quiet voice in her mind say, *Take the rest of the week off,* so she told her boss's receptionist that she would take the rest of the week off. It was Wednesday, which gave her three remaining days of the week.

After Cara hung up, Vicky said, "That was cool. I could hear you, and your boss's secretary. Are you really going back to work on Monday?"

"Yes."

Vicky was silent a moment. Then she asked, "Cara, how old are you?"

"I'm twenty-seven. How old are you?"

"I'm five."

"*Oh.*"

"I used to be four, then I had birthday, and now I'm five. Soon I'll be six."

"Nice."

Vicky became serious, "Cara, can I ask you something?"

"Yes."

"Why do people do bad things to other people?"

"Do you know the story of Adam and Eve?" Cara asked.

"I think so, didn't they do wrong against God, and He kicked them out of a garden?"

"Close, the Bible tells us that God told Adam and Eve that they could eat from any tree in the Garden of Eden, except for one. That tree was the tree of knowledge of good and evil which God told them not to eat from, lest they die. But the snake told Eve..."

Vicky injected, "The snake told Eve she would be like God, knowing good and evil. But the snake lied to her, and said she wouldn't die. So she ate some fruit from the tree, and shared some with Adam. But they did die, didn't they Cara?"

"They did indeed."

"Then they looked and saw they were naked. Then God told them they had to leave because they didn't follow God's orders."

"Yes," Cara agreed, "that's when sin, death, pain, and suffering entered the world."

"So why do people do bad things to other people?"

"People do bad things to other people because they choose to do bad things. You see, Vicky, everyone has free will, some choose to do bad things with it and some choose to do good things. But we all have the ability to choose. Those who follow God through Jesus Christ get rewarded in Heaven, those who don't choose to follow God through Jesus Christ, get punished in eternal damnation."

"Why would anyone choose to do something they knew was wrong, especially if they feel bad for doing it?"

"I don't know," Cara said frankly.

They were silent for a few minutes.

Then Cara turned into the community of Sellwood. There were small stores that lined the street on both sides. The road they were on was a two-lane road with bike paths on the outer edges.

"What city is this?" Vicky asked.

"This is Sellwood," Cara informed her. Many stores were just opening for the day. The coffee shops were open especially for the morning commuters on their way to work.

"I like it."

"That's good."

"It's small."

"It is."

"It looks like a nice place to be."

"I guess so."

Cara drove on past the shops and on to an area where houses lined the streets.

Vicky pointed out a large tree, "That one looks really old."

Cara drove a little further, and Vicky pointed out another, "I bet that tree looks beautiful in the spring."

They drove further on to see trees in the middle of the road.

"Why do they put trees in the middle of the road like that?"

"I think they do it to divide the road with something that looks nice."

"Oh. Did you know my grandpa is a tall tree? I think he's a Douglas fir. He's taller than most buildings. I bet he's even taller than a skyscraper. I hear those are tall buildings."

"Have you ever seen a skyscraper?"

"Nope."

"They are tall."

"Hey, Cara, you know what? I want to be tree, a tall tree, just like my grandfather. Then I want to live in the forest with him. I would be surrounded by other Potted people."

"Hmm," Cara said thinking about a forest filled with people who turned into plants. Before Vicky she had never thought of trees having their own community.

"Do trees communicate with each other?" Cara asked.

"Yeah."

"What do trees say?"

"All kinds of things: squirrel alerts, mountains lions approach, bunny rabbits, people on trails. The goings on in a forest, you know. Did you know that older trees protect and look after younger trees?"

"I did not."

"Well, they do. A mommy or a daddy tree will give some of the air they draw in to their child. Then that child can grow tall like their parents. Young trees can't always get access to sunlight, so the parents have to help."

"That's interesting; I did not know that before."

"Did you know that plants communicate with scents? It's really cool. Plants can also hear music and rhythms. At home, I sing to the plants as I water them. They seem to like my singing to them."

"That's really nice. Are there a lot of plants where you live? I mean, do your parents own land?"

"Yes, there are a lot of plants on the big land. My parents make other peoples' land look nice. They use rocks, trees, bushes, and some water. They never use Potted people, only plants that aren't people."

"Sounds like your parents are landscapers. That's a fitting career for a Potted Person."

"They have a business called 'LawnScapes.' I like when they do ponds. They did one pond that was so big; it took up an entire yard, and it was a *big* yard. It was bigger than this car, or your apartment. It was fun! When it was done, I got to see it, and I saw fish swimming in it. I like to see fish swimming."

"I like them too."

"Did you know that my siblings don't go to school? I don't go to school either because our parents teach us."

"They do?"

"Yep."

Then Vicky asked, "Do you ever think about Heaven?"

"Sometimes."

"I think about it a lot. I know it will be good. I have felt God with me, and Heaven is God's home. My dad says there's nothing bad in Heaven. It will be perfect, and I will be given a new body."

"It will be wonderful," Cara remarked thinking about when she died someday and went to Heaven.

Vicky continued, "I know God loves me."

"I know he loves me too."

Then Vicky began to sing, "Jesus loves me," and when she finished both were silent.

Vicky said after a bit, "I know God loves me, because he sent me to you. Because he wouldn't have sent me to you, if you were a bad person."

Cara was silent as she pondered that.

Cara turned onto a twisty road. Vicky threw her arms up in the air, "Cara, you're car is like a roller coaster. Wee!" she exclaimed.

Cara smiled at her in the rearview mirror, and then she returned her attention to the road.

"We are getting closer to the rhododendron garden, and I would like you to stay by my side as much as you can. If we find your parents, you're free to go with them, but if not, you must stay with me."

"Okay."

Cara made a sharp turn left, and drove another half mile until they saw a sign for the Crystal Springs Rhododendron Garden. Cara turned into the small parking lot. Cara unbuckled her seatbelt.

"This is a big garden, so I would like you to be careful and stay close to me."

"Yes ma'am!"

After a few more seconds, Cara stepped out and Vicky got out as well. Cara grabbed Vicky's hand, and they walked across the parking lot to the gate. They were greeted by cool air, and the sound of ducks and birds.

At the gate, there was a woman with long white hair tied in a low ponytail.

"One adult, and one child under eight," Cara informed her.

"That'll be $8," the woman told Cara. Cara pulled a twenty out of her purse. The woman put the twenty in the cash box, and pulled out change.

"Did you know that I'm a princess? At least my daddy says so," Vicky said her hands on the shelf at the bottom of the window.

"Ah, are you?" the woman asked.

"Yep, my parents own a lot of land, and they're P..."

Cara pretended to laugh, "Didn't you want to see the ducks? I thought you said you wanted to see the ducks. Well, c'mon let's go!" Cara interrupted quickly before Vicky could tell the woman her parents were Potted people.

"Bye!" Vicky called out as Cara pulled her along into the garden.

When they were just starting down the path, Vicky demanded, "Why so fast?"

Cara slowed down her pace to a walk, "I'm sorry," she said, "but I want to go further in before I tell you," she said glancing nervously at the ticket booth.

She didn't know what it was, but she felt unease about being there.

She and Vicky walked a little bit further on in silence. The bushes around them were not in bloom at that point in time. They walked down to the man-made waterfall, and there Vicky turned to Cara and asked, "Can you tell me now?"

Cara sighed, looked around to make sure no one was close enough to hear them, and then she lowered herself to Vicky's level, "Yes. I don't want you to tell a stranger your secret. I don't know if they're safe."

"Even if they're Potted people?"

"Was she a Potted person? Do you know that for sure?"

Vicky nodded her head.

"Stick to your parents' rule, okay?"

"Even to Potted people?"

"If it's a person you don't know, yes."

"Okay."

Cara stood up, and they continued walking down the path. As they walked, Cara held Vicky's hand in her left hand. With her free hand, Vicky ran her fingers along branches and leaves that she could reach.

After a while, Vicky said, "There's no trace of them."

"What?" Cara said stopping in her tracks.

"They're not here. These plants don't know anything of plants being added to the park."

"You know that by..." Cara trailed off looking at the plants around them.

"Well, yeah. I can talk to plants. They know the temperature, plants coming in, that sort of thing."

"You can talk to plants, and you can turn into a plant," Cara shook her head. "There's a lot more to you than at first glance. I hope I can learn it all."

They started to walk again, Vicky running her hand along branches, "You can it's easy. I can do most things a girl my age can do."

"Like what? What can you do?"

"I can run, walk, jump, skip, leap, and dance. See I can leap," Vicky demonstrated her ability to leap by jumping as far as she could along the path, which was about four feet.

When she jumped she had let go of Cara's hand, so she grabbed her hand once more, and they walked on.

"You certainly can," Cara said.

"The only thing is, I don't eat. At least like you do, I absorb energy from the sun. I do drink water, though."

"You don't eat?"

"Nope. I absorb sunlight."

"Okay. Do I need to know anything else? Is there anything else different?"

There was almost no one else around, because it was still early in the morning for a day that was going to be hot. They made their way to stairs cut into the ground, descending further down into the garden. They walked down to a duck pond. The pond was filled with algae floating on the surface. They watched as ducks and geese made trails in the grime as they swam about. Both Vicky and Cara watched the water fowl with some fascination. Then Vicky started running her hand along bushes around them.

"They're definitely not here," Vicky informed her.

"Do you want to go?"

"Yeah. I know my parents will find me."

Cara led them to the stairs. "How do you know your parents will find you?"

They walked up the stairs, and Vicky ran her hand along branches.

"I just..." she started to say, then she jerked her gaze to the path ahead of them, and she dove into some bushes nearby, turning into a young rhodie bush.

"That was w..." Cara started to say, and then she heard men's voices coming from the direction Vicky had jerked her head. They were walking toward Cara. She remained where she was, not sure what to do. Then Cara listened to their voices.

*Wait a minute...*she thought.

They came around the corner, and Cara waved to them.

"Ron, Ted, hi!"

The two men came a little closer, "Cara, you're here on a weekday morning?" the one with dark hair, Ted asked.

"Yeah, I decided to take time off from work. I think I need it, and I certainly had some vacation saved up." As she talked to them she was careful not to mention Vicky because at the back of her mind, she wondered if these were the men who separated Vicky from her parents.

"You certainly did. Still it is good to see you here, at this time. Not to mention strange," Ted said.

"It's not as strange as seeing you two here. Why are you guys here?" Cara asked looking between them both.

At her question Ron began to look uncomfortable, but Ted didn't seem to be bothered.

"We were nearby. We're on a personal errand."

"What kind of errand?" Cara asked, her heart rate speeding up as she thought about what that could be.

"We...uh...um...are looking for ..."Ted stuttered.

Ron moved out of her sight. Cara wasn't able to see Ron emphatically shake his head and wave his arms.

"For? For what?" Cara demanded, and then adjusted where she was to see them both. Ron stopped moving and stood still.

"What are you looking for?" she insisted.

Ted sighed, "For a little girl. She's about six or seven, she's lost, and we're trying to find her."

Cara's heart dropped, "A little girl?" she asked trying to remain calm, even though there was a storm in her chest.

"Since when are you two in the child retrieval business?" she asked more hotly than she intended. At her reaction both men backed up a step away from her.

"Her parents are looking for her, and we thought we could help," Ted said.

"How did you two get involved?"

Ron answered, "We were in the right place, at the right time."

"Okay, then," Cara said, "I should go, I was on my way out. I'll see you two on Monday."

"Bye," Ron said as they started walking down the path, moving closer to her.

They passed her, and then Ted turned to her, "You'll tell us if you see her? She has very vivid eyes."

No, I will not! Cara thought, but she said, "I don't know."

"Why not?" Ted asked.

"Because I...I would want to do the right thing. I would want to do the safest thing for the child." Cara hoped her answer did not reveal how much she knew, and that they were satisfied enough to leave.

Ron said, "Alright."

They walked on. After they were gone and out of earshot Cara let out a sigh of relief. She could feel her heart pounding in her ears. It was like a stare down, and if she had turned away or backed down, she would've lost and so would've Vicky.

She whispered, "Vicky, to my side quickly."

The young rhodie turned back into to a girl, and walked out of the bush she had dived into. She looked shaken and about ready to cry.

"Cara..." she whispered.

Cara put a finger to her lips, and then she pointed up the path toward the entrance. Then thinking she came off as too harsh she whispered, "We'll talk about it in my car on the way home, okay?"

Vicky nodded her head.

"Good, let's go," Cara looked around them, and then they started running toward the entrance. The paths sloped downward into the garden, but they sloped uphill to exit. It slowed their progress some, but before they knew it, they were at the entrance, then racing past it and toward Cara's car. Cara got her keys out, and pressed the unlock button on the remote. Cara got into her seat, and Vicky got into her car seat in the back.

"Buckle up," Cara told her as she buckled her own seatbelt. Vicky clicked the buckle.

Cara turned on the ignition and hit the reverse.

Thank you, Father, for a small parking lot, where I can get to my car quickly, she said silently as she switched it to drive and drove out.

Then she said just as silently, *this is going to be rough.* Her car was normally driven at the speed limit or just below, but when she pulled out of the parking lot, she was fuelled by adrenaline and so she drove a bit faster.

After a bit, though, she didn't see either of their cars tailing her, so she was able to calm down and drive slower.

Right about that time, Vicky said, "You know the men who separated me from my parents."

"I thought I knew them," she said. "They're my coworkers, which means I work with them. Vicky, I didn't know about this, at all. When you came to me,

I had never even heard of Potted people, let alone, that they existed."

"I believe you," she said.

Cara glanced at Vicky in the rearview mirror, then back to the road, "You do?" she asked surprised.

"Yeah, I trust you. I told you God wouldn't have led me to you if you were a bad person. I know God won't let me down. He will guide and protect me, and He led me to you."

Vicky's words of faith in God and in Cara went right to Cara's heart, touching deeply. Vicky had faith that would stand.

Wow, God, Cara prayed, *help me to have faith like Vicky. Thank you for bringing her to me.*

Then she heard in her mind, *Don't worry for I am with you. I will help you through this event/challenge. Do not fear.*

Then Vicky thought for a moment, and then she said, "I think the fact that you know those men, is why God sent me to you."

Cara was silent as she pondered that.

Cara drove on in silence. Vicky was silent for the rest of the trip. When they arrived at Cara's apartment complex, Cara parked, and then they ran up the stairs to Cara's apartment. Then Cara bolted and latched the door closed behind them. They collapsed onto the couch.

"What now, Cara?" Vicky asked.

"Now, we pray," Cara said.

"Okay."

Cara grabbed Vicky's hands, and they bowed their heads and closed their eyes.

"God, please help me. Don't let those men find Vicky. Give me wisdom, and be my strength. Don't let Vicky fall. Help me to know what to do. In Jesus's name, Amen."

Then Vicky started to pray, "Dear God, thank you for leading me to Cara. Thank you for always keeping watch over me. Please help Cara to keep me safe. In Jesus's name *I* pray, Amen."

"Amen!" Cara exclaimed. They both opened their eyes. Cara enjoyed listening to Vicky pray. To hear a child pray is a tender and sweet moment to be treasured, and Cara did just that.

There was still the question of what to do. Then, Vicky asked, "Can we go see grandpa's tree?"

"Where does he live?"

"Center Washington, my parents showed me on a map once."

"How far away is that?"

"Less than a day away."

Cara grabbed her phone out of her purse. She brought up Google Maps, and had Vicky show her where it was. Cara put in her address, and the directions showed a 5 1/2 hour drive.

"Are you sure?" she asked.

"Yes, my grandfather is really nice. You'd like him."

"I bet I would."

"A drive would be good. We'd get away from these men for the day. Please?"

"If we start now, and then turn around and come back, we'd be driving back in the hottest time of day. But if we start out early tomorrow morning, we have more cool times we'd be travelling."

"Woo-hoo!" Vicky exclaimed.

"That means 1 or 2 in the morning."

"Okay."

"So, I'll need to go to bed early tonight, and we should get a bag of potting soil, as well as food items for me and water for each of us. We'll have to go shopping later today."

Cara liked to have a plan, to know where she was going. The plan was set, they would be leaving early, and travel for most of the day.

4

A TRIP TO WASHINGTON

Everything was set and ready to go when Cara got up at 12:30. The day before, they had gone to the store and bought items like snacks, water bottles, extra potting soil, and some activity books for Vicky along with some crayons for the ride home. The evening before Cara had put everything into her car, so that they could leave as early as possible. That way, she only had to carry down Vicky's pot.

Before Cara carried Vicky's pot down to her car, she made a quick breakfast of microwave scrambled eggs, slices of toast, a slice of sandwich cheese, and some deli meat. She finished everything off quickly, and left the dishes in the sink.

Then she walked over to the small flowering tree near the door, she opened the door, then she lowered herself to a squatting position, wrapped her arms around the pot and stood up using her knees to lift instead of her back. The pot weighed about 20-30 pounds with soil and tree in it. Cara placed the pot as softly as she could outside her door. She locked her door, and carried the pot carefully down the stairs. Cara carried the pot on her right side, so she could see the stairs. At the bottom, Cara set the pot on the ground.

She unlocked the doors, and she lifted the pot slowly and carefully into her car. She made sure to set the pot on the plastic plate on the floor of her car. Then she poured some water from a watering can onto the soil. In that moment, it seemed that the tree relaxed some by the branches spreading out; it was as if Vicky was saying, "Ahh," with a contented sigh.

"I'm glad you liked that. I will try to make the ride a comfortable one for you. I'll try to make it so you don't lose soil."

Cara closed the door, and got in her door. She buckled her seatbelt, and put the keys into the ignition. Before every long trip she prayed, so she paused a moment to offer aloud a prayer.

"Dear God, please lead us today. Protect us on this journey today, and just be with us. I thank you that you are already on the road. You go before us and you're behind us and with us. Help us in all things we encounter today. In Jesus' name I pray, amen. I also seek you this morning."

She drove out of the apartment complex, and as she turned onto the main thoroughfare, she could feel Vicky's agreement with everything she prayed.

The streets were quiet at a quarter after one in the morning. There was about one car every five seconds and sometimes two. Cara was able to drive farther faster, because the traffic was so light. All lights were green. It was different seeing her town at that time in the morning: there were no buses, no pedestrians, no bicyclists, and only the twenty-four hour convenience stores were open.

She drove north to Portland. She looked for any sign of Ron or Ted's car. The roads were open, and when she reached the interstate without seeing any sign of them, she was able to relax. She started to breathe more normal.

Cara started to reflect on her life to that point. One thought that occurred the morning before, was coming up. This time, it was like a light beam highlighted it, and it stood out clearly. There was a certain word: passion. She felt like her life was missing passion. The kind of passion where a woman who is serving in Africa as a missionary and who also likes evenings over mornings can't wait to get up in the morning because she loves being there so much. It's like your life is an adventure story, written just for you, and you can't wait to see what happens next. It doesn't mean there won't be bad days; it means that the good and the bad make the adventure an adventure.

It was an inspiring thought, and Cara could feel the excitement rising. It described the passion Cara wanted in her life.

Passion is an important attribute in life. But as Cara soon realized, she wanted to shine in God's light and live to glorify God just as much as she wanted passion. Cara had an image in her mind of her as a lighthouse, and Jesus was the lighthouse Keeper who was working in her and through her to shine forth to those trapped upon the dark seas. Of course, she couldn't shine without the lighthouse Keeper's constant work. It was his work in her that gave her light and life.

Grace is beautiful, she thought. Then she was silent as she was drove.

God is the greatest light, and his glory is greater than anything. Cara thought about God using her to touch others' lives. When she was in elementary, she had talked to her friends about what it meant to be a Christian. She had been so excited to be used by God. Her heart felt lighter.

Then she wondered, *What happened? How did I get down so far?*

At that point in her life, it felt as dark as the world around her. Thinking of the oncoming dawn, she was filled with hope. Besides, after the dark, there is always light. It's the same in the spiritual life, the dark is banished by the light, and then darkness appears, then light once more. Darkness is limited, there's nothing beyond pitch black, but there can always be more light.

Cara enjoyed the vast time she had to think. It was a luxury to drive in the early hours of the morning. It was dark on the open road, but the sky was a burgundy color that promised a new day. There was hope in that.

She started to think about how God in her life was an easy burden, which made things easier. If her life was like a cup and God was the pitcher, then he poured out his Sprit, the Holy Spirit, into the cup. The cup could be full to overflowing but it never weighed anything. But it refreshed her more than water. The Holy Spirit also refueled her better than any food. In the times she felt low, even beyond what she could handle, that's when he showed his great love to her. Sometimes, it was bringing a friend into her life, or in some moments meeting her where she was with a Bible verse, a song, a journal entry she had written, or a memory that showed God's love for her.

The road stretched beyond what Cara could see, and it seemed to be a metaphor for her life. The road seemed to represent where she came from and where she was going, all the twists and turns in the road and the car was the way of getting through it all. The distance between A and B was hundreds of miles, and her car was a tiny percentage of that. Her life was measured in years, not miles.

The best part was that she had God to share her burdens with. If she felt overwhelmed she had someone to confide in. If she was lost, she had a comforter who was always by her side, and she could always count on him. It was her greatest joy when she was frustrated to be able to look up. She could give her struggles to God. God was her source of strength and peace. That peace she gained could be shared. When she shared it, others would find God's peace for their lives. When they found God's peace, it would be great joy to her. In that case, it would be a gift for others as well as for her.

Cara thought about all the people who looked for peace outside of God. Here heart ached for them because anything that wasn't God would only satisfy them for a moment and could never give them what they truly longed for. Even what they were designed to hunger and thirst for: a relationship with their Creator. Cara had a few people in mind she wished could experience God's grace.

Cara was reminded of when Jesus said, "I am the light of the world. He who follows Me shall not walk in darkness, but have the light of life." (John 8:12)

Cara thought of the verse, "Your word is a lamp unto my feet, and a light unto my path." (Psalms 119:105) She realized it was just like the headlights on her car illuminating the road before her. Her lights did not show the full length of road that was shown when the sun was up, but the headlights showed her enough to drive at the speed she would in the daytime.

She loved when things just clicked. Verses she had read for years or memorized when she was in school, she suddenly understood what they meant, or details that she had missed before stood out. As God gave her a whole new insight into what she was reading.

It's wonderful, she thought. Then a shiver went up her spine, and goose bumps rose on her arms as she felt a soft rush of cool air pass by her.

Thank you, Father God, she said silently. It was such a sweet and tender moment; she started to think of how wonderfully sweet it was to feel God with her. His presence filled her with a calm and gentle peace, a quiet for her soul that was truly comforting. In those moments she could feel brightness in her eyes, and she longed for more. There was a hunger in her soul, which would only be satisfied with God.

For God satisfied her soul, and made her dwell in his good grace.

In Proverbs 4:18-19 it says, "But the path of the just is like the shining sun, that shines even brighter unto the perfect day. The way of the wicked is like darkness; they do not know what makes them stumble."

Her heart was being filled in a way she had needed for a long time. It felt good, like cool, refreshing water on the hottest day of summer.

I want to be a blessing, she thought.

She started to think about the plant in the back. The young girl was riding smoothly. Vicky loved God, and she loved her family. Cara started to wonder what kind of person she would be as she grew up. Would she be as passionate about God as she was when she stayed with Cara? What would she be like?

It was at that moment that Cara realized that the sky was getting brighter. There was sliver of golden light on the hills to her right. The strip of golden light turned into a sunrise of pinks, purples, and oranges that filled the sky on her right side. The sunrise was beautiful, and within minutes the sun was up.

Then Cara heard leaves moving, and branches shifting. Then she heard a yawn, "Morning."

Cara looked up surprised at the rearview mirror. There was Vicky standing there in the pot with soil up to her calves.

"Buckle up," Cara told her.

Vicky sat down on the seat, and buckled the seatbelt around her.

"Where are we?" she asked.

"We are half an hour from where you said your grandpa lives."

"Cara, I'm so excited, you get to meet my mom's dad! He's one of my favorite people in the world. If he's a tree, I'll talk to him for you. If he's not, then you get to talk to him for you. I hope he knows where my parents are."

"What if he hasn't seen them?"

"Uh..."

"Then we'll have to go back to my house. Let's not worry about that right now, just tell me when you recognize where we enter. Then point it out to me, and I'll stop the car."

Vicky was silent as she watched out the passenger side window. Then just half an hour later, as Cara had said, Vicky exclaimed, "Cara, I know those trees!"

"Is that it?" Cara asked.

Vicky was bouncing in her seat, "It is. That's the place where my brother, sister, mom, and dad and I enter. That's the place!"

Cara pulled her car over to the side of the road in a space big enough for her car to safely pull over.

"Are we okay?" Cara asked.

"Yep, this is where we enter. This is where we park."

Cara turned off the engine. "All right then." She had driven straight through for five and a half hours, and she was ready to stretch her legs.

She grabbed a backpack, and her jacket. There was a breeze rustling the leaves adding a chill to the air. She zipped her jacket all the way up.

For now, she thought. She reached for Vicky's brand-new coat. She held it open for her, and Vicky slipped her arms in.

Cara swung the straps of her backpack over her shoulders.

"Are you ready?" she asked.

"Yep!" Vicky exclaimed bouncing with excitement.

"Well, lead on," Cara instructed her.

Vicky walked to the row of trees, her head held high, and her arms swinging at her sides. She walked between two trees and Cara followed.

Inside, she saw many more trees, and ferns covering the ground and her ankles. The forest was mostly in shade, except for a few beams of sunlight shining to the forest floor. It was so peaceful, that Cara drew in a deep breath and let it out in a contented sigh. As they hiked in, the sounds of the city became fainter.

Cara watched Vicky as she started to get some distance on her. Vicky was so natural in the forest; she was just so...graceful. She moved like a pageantry girl: as if she was floating.

Once or twice, Cara thought she saw small roots in the path lower themselves as they passed through. It was so amazing that Cara stopped to watch it a few times. The world of the Potted people still seemed so strange and new for Cara, and it was taking time to get used to.

To Vicky, on the other hand, it was as normal as breathing or as natural as a polar bear in the arctic. To her, it wasn't strange at all. Rather, a "normal" person was odd to her. Cara laughed a little as she thought, *What is normal, anyways? If everyone is different, than how could there be a "normal"?*

Normal, she rationalized, is just a standard. In order to have a standard, you must have a set of rules to define what that standard was.

She paused to look up at the trees. She felt a little dizzy looking up at them. She soon realized that every tree was different, even among the same kinds. From the signature of their bark, to the number of their rings: they were all made to be different.

Just like people, Cara thought. *God, you made all people to be different; each with their own talents, gifts, and desires; and you have a plan for all of us.* Despite the cold, she felt a little warmer. God had made her to fit into her own niche, she just didn't know where that was, yet.

She looked ahead at Vicky; she was climbing over a small pile of rocks. Cara tightened the straps on her backpack, before she walked over to the pile. She stepped carefully onto the lower rocks. She walked up the rock slope. At the top of it, she had to pause to catch her breath. She looked back at all the land they had traversed thus far. It was about two or three miles by her estimation.

"Are you okay, Cara?" Vicky asked.

"Yeah, just catching my breath and admiring the view."

"Okay," Vicky said. Then she looked at her and asked, "Are you ready to go?"

"Yeah," Cara replied.

Vicky started walking once more, and Cara followed. Vicky placed her hand on the trunk of a tree, nodded her head, then gestured to Cara, "This way, Cara," she directed.

Cara followed Vicky through the trees. A little further on, the ground sloped sharply for about five feet down. There were roots interlacing, and serving as stairs.

"Thank you, trees," Cara said aloud. In that moment, she saw the tops of some bow almost imperceptibly.

"Wow," she whispered. She reached the bottom, and she started hurrying to catch up to Vicky. The ground on the last few two hundred feet was mostly flat. Then they stepped into a clearing. The sun lit up the clearing. The first thing Cara noticed was a big hole on the opposite side of them.

Vicky stopped and started looking around nervously.

"Is this..." Cara began.

Vicky nodded her head. Cara had a hard time discerning if she was excited or concerned that her grandpa's tree was not where it ought to be.

"Where could he..." Cara started to ask.

Then they both heard someone whistling as he or she was coming from the trail near the hole. They each stood there listening. He was getting closer to them. Then he emerged from the trees and was standing across from them.

"Grandpa!" Vicky exclaimed running up to him and giving him a big hug. He was tall, about six feet at least with a grey and white beard that went down to his chest. He had on a long sleeve red flannel shirt, blue jeans, and hiking boots. He reached down and picked up his granddaughter.

"Vicky, I'm glad to see you. Where is your family?"

"Aren't they here?"

"No, I haven't seen them."

"Oh. We were hoping they'd be here."

"Wait, who's 'we'?"

Vicky pointed to Cara, "Her. Her and me."

He shifted Vicky to his side, to see Cara standing there.

"Hello there," he told her.

"Hello," Cara echoed.

"How did you get here?" he inquired.

"Your granddaughter led me here. She was..."

"I was separated from mom and dad in Oregon, and God lead me to her."

"He did?"

"Yes sir, and then she took me in, and she's watched me since."

"How did you become separated from your parents? What happened?"

"Well, mom and I went into a store and when men showed up mom told me to hide. The next thing I knew they were gone, and God was telling me to leave the store. Those men were the kinds who were after me."

"Then God lead you to her..." He looked at Cara. Cara stood there awkwardly not knowing what to do or if she needed to say anything. The best thing to do, she supposed was to stand there quietly.

Then he asked her, "What's your name?"

"I'm Cara Stenfeld."

"She knows the men who separated me from my parents," Vicky added in.

Cara turned a little pink.

"Is this true?" Vicky's grandfather asked her.

"It is, sir."

Feeling braver Cara added, "They're my coworkers, where I work. I've worked with them for six years. I had no way of knowing they were involved in this."

"Miss Stenfeld," he said, "would you like to go talk privately with me?"

Cara's gaze had fallen down to the ground, and when she looked up into his blue eyes she did not expect to see the love and compassion she saw there. Her posture lost its rigidity, and she was able to relax a bit.

Cara wanted to talk to someone more than anything, but she had one concern, "What about Vicky? Is she going to be all right here?"

"Don't worry about her, she's safe. Besides, here, she knows how to protect herself. Don't you?"

"Yep."

"See. She'll be fine, I assure you. She's much safer here."

He set Vicky on her feet.

"Come, Cara," he told her walking down the path he had come from. She followed him down to a brook that gurgled over some rocks. The brook brought the temperature down several degrees. The brook was a pleasant background noise. They could talk in peace without being easily overheard, but they were still near enough that they could run back if something happened.

There were a few large boulders near the creek, Vicky's grandpa took the one on the right side, and Cara took one on the left. She took off the backpack on her shoulders and set it down at her feet.

It felt good to take a break.

"Tell me about the men who separated my grand-daughter from my daughter and son-in-law. Who are they?"

In Vicky's grandpa's eyes, Cara didn't see any harsh-ness, no anger, no hatred, just a pure, honest desire to know about the men who separated his beloved grand-daughter from her parents. Vicky's grandpa's posture and tone of voice let Cara know that she could trust him. He wasn't out to condemn her, but rather, to be an encourager to her. There was a pain in Cara's eyes, and what Cara didn't know was that his heart ached for her. She appeared to be few years younger than his daughter. Indeed she was not Lily, Cara was shorter with brown hair instead of red, but he could see the same headstrong attitude in Cara that Lily possessed. At the end of the day, though, they were still girls who needed their dads. Like Vicky, he reasoned to himself. All three—Cara, Vicky, and Lily—needed their dads.

He listened as Cara spoke, "The two men are Ron and Ted, and Vicky said they want to use her ability to gather information, and thankfully it seems they don't know what she looks like."

"How well did you know those men?" he asked.

"I thought I knew them pretty well," Cara eyes started to tear up. "I babysat their kids...when they would go out on date nights. I...I knew...I knew their families."

Cara cried with tears flowing down her cheeks, as emotions started stirring that she hadn't been able to deal with.

"There, there. It's okay," he said putting a hand on her shoulder.

After a moment she said, "Do you want to know what gets me upset? What really gets me? What kind of example are they being for their kids? What are they teaching them? That it's okay to lie, cheat, steal, kidnap, and use and abuse. I am beyond mad, I am absolutely livid. This is not okay, no matter their reasons. What they're doing is horrendous and awful. Ted has a son who has a lot of medical bills, but that doesn't make it right. It just makes me sick. I wonder if their wives know."

Cara was silent a moment. She needed to vent, and Vicky's grandpa let her. It was such a relief to unload the heavy, emotional burden from her shoulders. It was just like her setting her backpack at her feet.

She continued, "I guess you can see that I'm angry, but I'm also sad for them. This evil will start them down a path that with be very hard to turn from. I also wonder how far gone they are."

Vicky's grandpa rubbed his chin, and then he spoke, "It seems to me, Cara," he said slowly, carefully as if picking his words, "that those men, who were friends of yours, have now left a hurt in your heart. Have you given them up to God?"

Cara shook her head.

"Only he can save them. Only God can redeem them. Let us pray."

They turned to face each other, bowed their heads and closed their eyes.

"Father God, your desire is that 'none may perish, but all may experience everlasting life,' that's why you sent your son Jesus to die for us. God, we give you these men, their wives and their children. We know that they are all precious in your sight. Help these men to know you are God. God, you didn't send your son into the world to condemn it, but by Jesus it would be saved. That's what we ask: save these men.

"Father, I thank you for what Cara is doing to protect my granddaughter. I am so amazed and utterly astounded at what she is doing for my family. Please help her as she continues to protect Vicky, and don't let her fall. Please be with her and guide her as she goes on this journey. Give her wisdom, and give her peace. We pray that you would strengthen her resolve in you. In Jesus's name, we pray, amen."

"Amen," Cara repeated, opening her eyes. "You're welcome," she said. "Thank you for praying for me."

"I meant every word I said. Cara, what you're doing is honorable. It's not every day we have a non-potted person person help us out. Things are about to get much harder. You're in a position where you will have to make a choice between them or Vicky. You won't be able to have it both ways."

"I have already promised Vicky that I would protect her with my whole self, and I meant it. I will do the right thing, even if that means great personal loss for me."

"I figured as much, but you still need to know that it won't be easy. The road ahead will be hard to travel on. I know God will bless you, not just now, but down the road. The truth is, I can never say thank you, enough. I am blessed that there are still people in the world like you who are willing to do the right thing."

"I love her as if she was my own daughter, and I will do everything I can to see that she is reunited with her parents. Your granddaughter is an incredible little girl, who has a heart for God."

He smiled, "She certainly does."

"I love that about her."

"Me too."

"I only hope that Ron and Ted's kids will know God's grace in their lives. It's still hard, because I will always remember tucking their kids into bed with bedtime stories, hugs, and hot chocolate. Ron and Ted trusted me with their children, and I, in turn, trusted them as well. I know things will never be the same with either of them, and I might not have the same relationship with their families. I will do whatever it takes to protect your granddaughter, because I am no quitter, and I will keep her from them.

The only thing is, I have to go in to work on Monday, and I'll have to face them with what I now know."

Vicky's grandpa asked, "What are you thinking about that?"

"I'm a little scared, and I hope I don't jeopardize protecting Vicky. I'm overwhelmed as well, and I've even thought about postponing going back to work. If I do go back, I'll have to find a sitter. I don't know who I can trust."

"Continue to ask for God's help. I'll be praying for God to keep you both safe. As far as Monday goes, you need to go back; you need to watch every move they make. But before we go I want you know something."

"Yes?"

"When I first looked into your eyes, I saw pain in them, and they looked dim. But in that moment after we prayed, I saw God's light starting to shine forth. I see why God has chosen you to watch Vicky and keep her safe. You love God, too."

"Thank you, sir."

"I mean it, 'Let you light so shine before men, that they may see your good works and glorify your Father in Heaven.' I have faith in you, and I trust you to trust God to help you make the right decisions."

"Thank you, sir."

"Shall we go?"

Cara grabbed her backpack, and they walked back up the trail. They were forty feet away when they stopped, and listened to Vicky speaking.

"...I like her, she's nice. She's like an aunt or a cousin to me. She's human, and I love her. Did you know she has an apartment and she drives a car? I know, because I am staying with her in her apartment and I ride in her car. I know she loves God, but she is far away from Him."

As Cara listened she thought *Wow, God, is she on the right track, or what? To think that even a child can see I'm far from you, God. But Vicky is unlike any child I've ever met.*

89

Cara and Vicky's grandfather stood there a moment longer without saying a word as Vicky talked to the trees around her.

Then they both emerged from their hiding spot, and Vicky looked up at them. She was sitting cross-legged on the ground.

"Cara, Grandpa!" she exclaimed.

She jumped up from her position on the ground, and threw her arms around Cara's waist.

"I was just talking about you to the trees. You know they're really good listeners."

Cara and Vicky's grandpa exchanged a glance, "We know," Cara replied, "we heard you as were coming up the trail. I think it's time we started to go back to my home."

"But, Cara, I want us to stay a little bit longer. Maybe leave tomorrow?"

"Vicky, I can't stay here. I don't have a place to sleep. You have a place to stay, you can turn into a tree, but I can't. Do you understand what I'm saying?"

"Yeah. But maybe you and I could...could visit again, sometime?"

"Another time, after your parents find you."

"OK! Did you hear that grandpa? She's coming back to see you with me and my parents. Then we can all be together!"

A smile lit up his face, "I think she meant that at a later time, but not right away."

"Oh," Vicky said. "But it will happen!"

"Yes," Vicky's grandpa said.

She flung her arms around her grandfather, "I love you," she whispered into his ear. He clutched her tighter.

"I love you too, Little Flower. Come back with the rest of your family. I want to see them too."

Cara could see the bond between granddaughter and grandfather. He loved his granddaughter, and she loved him.

"Now, you've got to take Cara home. Can you do that for me?"

"Yeah."

"Good. Bye Vicky."

"Bye, Grandpa."

"Good-bye to you too, Cara Stenfeld. Thank you again. Don't ever give up, because God will see you through."

"I won't give up," Cara assured him. "Thank you for the prayer."

"Anytime," he said.

Cara and Vicky walked toward the path they had used to come in.

The first part was uphill, but most of the trail after that was downhill. Many places along their path were steep and had to be traversed carefully. At that point, the air was starting to become warmer.

Cara thought to herself, *Isn't it amazing how quickly it gets warm outside?*

Vicky then asked, "Do you want to know something that's amazing?"

"Sure," Cara replied.

Vicky slid off a log, "Well, did you know the word 'son' is spelled two ways: one spelling refers to the star in the sky, the other is a male child?"

"I did indeed," Cara replied climbing over the same log.

"Well, did you know that both kinds of 'sons' are good for you? As a Potted person, I can turn sunlight into energy, but I also need Jesus the Son of God everyday to have the strength to face the day."

"You need both variations of sunlight," Cara echoed thoughtfully. She started to think about the similarities between the two words. She had never thought about it that way, but the more she thought about it, the more she realized how right Vicky was. Even though she wasn't a Potted person, she too needed sunlight and she also needed to replenish her stores of Son light every day.

The way to do that was for her to read her Bible, and seek His face daily. In the good times and the bad, she needed God's guidance, and in order to receive that she had to focus on building a relationship with Him. He was always nearby and ready for her to come back to Him.

She realized she had not made the time to be with God.

I am sorry, God, she whispered. *Take me back, and help me to never put you on the back burner again. Be at the forefront of my mind and thoughts. Thank you, God that you haven't given up on me. I need you every minute of every day, without you I feel empty and lost.*

I am here, with you, she heard in her mind.

In the forest, she felt calm and a peace. The air was still fresh, cool, clean, and she breathed it in filling her lungs with good air.

The forest was a church with branches high above their heads acting like a stained glass windows in that they fragmented the light shining through them. The trees stood around them as a silent choir lifting their branches up as if in worship to their Creator.

As Cara drove home, she thought about these things, treasuring them in her heart.

5

TIME FOR FELLOWSHIP

Three days later, it was Sunday. Cara was asleep in her bed, when all of a sudden; Vicky belly flopped onto the bed.

"Wh...What is it?" Cara mumbled. Then she demanded, "Vicky, why did you do that?"

"C'mon Cara, it's Sunday, it's church day!"

Cara reached for her cell phone on the nightstand. She pushed the button on top to wake it up.

"Oh, it's eight in the morning. It starts in a little over an hour from now at nine-fifteen."

"Can we go, please Cara? I want to go to church."

"All right, yes, we'll go. But I need to get ready first."

"I'm ready, see?" she showed that she had on her new shoes.

"I do see."

"Cara, will you braid my hair?"

"Sure. I will braid your hair if you go grab my brush, and some hair ties from the bathroom."

Vicky hopped off the bed excitedly. From a few feet away Cara heard, "I see your brush, but where are the hair ties?"

Then Cara answered back, "They're in the drawer beneath the sink."

"Found them!"

Vicky came back into Cara's bedroom, brush in one hand, and small plastic bin of hair ties, in the other.

Cara let out a laugh, "You brought in all the hair ties?"

"Yep."

"Ok. Come on up here."

She set the bin and the brush at the foot of the bed, and then she jumped onto the bed. She sat in front of Cara, and Cara started to brush her hair out.

"I like that that feels nice."

Cara grabbed a hair tie, and started to brush her hair into a ponytail.

"That's good," Cara said.

"Did you know I've been here almost five days?"

Cara separated her hair into three strands.

Cara started to think back, calculating it in her mind, "Let's see that was Wednesday morning, and this is Sunday." Then she counted quietly to herself, and she said aloud. "Wow, I guess you're right, it *has* been five days."

"That's...that's almost a week isn't it?"

"Yeah, it is." One strand went over the middle. Another strand went over that one.

"So, I've been away from my family for almost a week, now?"

Cara was quiet for a moment, "That's right."

"So, what will a week from now look like?"

"I don't know," Cara admitted pausing. "Let's just take this one day at a time, okay? The best thing we can do is start with today."

"Okay, that sounds good."

"Besides if we spend our time looking at minutes, or worrying about the future, we lose that time, and it's gone forever. I guess there's some philosophy for you."

"Time is very...hard to describe, isn't it? Cara, how would you describe time?"

"Sometimes, it moves slowly, while other times it moves fast like a European bullet train."

"Yep, that works."

Cara looked up at the clock on the wall, "Speaking of time, it's time for me to get ready for church."

"Will you finish braiding my hair first?"

"Yes, and then I am going to take a shower, get breakfast, and get dressed."

"What will I do in the meantime?"

"Don't worry what you will do; I'm sure you will find something to do. You could color in one of the coloring books I bought you."

"Okay."

Cara finished braiding, and then she said, "There, you're done."

Vicky pulled the braid over her shoulder, "Thank you, Cara," she said hopping off the bed. She looked at her reflection in one of the closet doors.

"I like it," she said turning one way and then the other.

"I'm glad. Now, if you'll excuse me, I need to grab clothes."

"Oh, okay."

She stepped out of the way. "Can I help you choose?"

Cara opened one panel, "Yes, you may help me choose."

Vicky starred in. "Hmmm. Ooh, I like that!" she said pointing to a purple button-up blouse, that had three-quarters sleeves.

Cara pulled it out, "Good choice. That covers the shirt, but with this shirt I like to wear an undershirt."

Vicky did a quick scan, "Oh, wear that," she said pointing to a white camisole.

"Okay, now that the top half is taken care of, what do I wear on the bottom half?"

"Easy, that black skirt," she said pointing to a knee-length pencil skirt.

Cara pulled the camisole and the skirt from her closet.

"You're pretty good at this. What about shoes?"

"Thank you. Um, for shoes..." she stepped into the closet, closer to Cara's shoe collection.

Vicky held up a pair of black wedges, "These," she said.

"Okay, thank you. I'll try to hurry up.'"

She grabbed the wedges out of Vicky's hand.

"Are you going to be alright?"

"Yep," Vicky replied popping her "p". Cara walked to the bathroom, with Vicky in tow. Cara went into the bathroom to hang her clothes up, and Vicky went into the living room, grabbing her coloring books and box of crayons off the coffee table. Vicky lay down on the floor, and opened her coloring book to the next blank page.

Cara watched Vicky make her crayon selection, and start coloring. As she colored she turned her head.

"Are you sure, you're going to be alright?" Cara asked from the bathroom.

"Yes," she replied without looking up.

Even though the bathroom door opened into the living room area, she still kept it open a crack to listen for anything. After a while, she closed it all the way.

God, thank you for Vicky, she is quite a treasure.

Cara started to pray: *God, I'm sorry for not going to church the last year and a half. Thank you for opening my eyes so I can see. Draw me to your side. Help me to remember the lessons I'm learning this week. In Jesus' name I pray, amen.*

She felt God's presence, and a new thought occurred to her, *Whatever I learn this week will completely change my life.*

You got it, she heard the quiet voice in her mind say. She was able to catch her reflection in the mirror above the sink. She saw a confidence growing within her; a might. Her shoulders were back and her head was held high. God was reconstructing her heart. He was replanting her in Jesus, so that she could bear much fruit.

God was moving in her life, creating in her a desire for Him, which cannot be quenched. He was breathing on the flame of her soul, reigniting it. The fire for God was the passion she was craving in her life. She had needed God.

She thought about Vicky coloring in the living room. Her passion for God was contagious.

Help me to be more like her, she prayed quickly.

She stepped into the shower. Once she was underneath the warm pressure of the water, she was able to relax some. But she still made it faster than normal. The shower felt wonderful. Afterward, she felt refreshed: there is nothing better than the joy of being clean spiritually, emotionally, or physically. It's like having a weight lifted, that you've carried for a long, long, time.

In the moment before putting her make-up on, or putting her hair up, Cara felt beautiful. Her skin had a healthy glow to it.

God, thank you for this moment, she said silently.

She put on the outfit that Vicky helped her pick out. Vicky had done a good job. The colors worked out well together. She kept her make-up minimal, and her hair she put up into a bun.

When she stepped out she asked Vicky, "How are you doing, still ok?"

"Uh-huh," Vicky replied.

She went into the kitchen to make a meal for herself. All the while, Vicky colored quietly. Cara was rushing to get ready for church, and Vicky was waiting calmly and patiently. Cara stopped for a moment to ponder this. In the Bible, there is the story of Mary and Martha. Jesus was at their house, and while Martha served, Mary sat at Jesus' feet listening to His word. Cara was like Martha in that moment, and Vicky was like Mary. Cara was running around like Martha, but what she needed was a moment to be still in Jesus' presence like Vicky or Mary. How did Cara get to be so far from God? She simply did not take the moments to be still in God's presence.

God isn't only for emergencies or when times are good. God is for the everyday moments. To build a relationship, you wouldn't only call on someone when you needed them would you?

Cara wanted a new direction in her life, and she could learn a few things from Vicky who loved God with her entire soul. The thing about Vicky, she was either hot or cold, she either liked something or she didn't, and there wasn't a lot of in-between. All in or not at all, that's how Vicky lived. If there was a puddle, she was either all wet or completely dry. Cara, it seemed, could learn a lot from Vicky. She was very often like a ship adrift upon the sea, being blown about by the wind. Vicky made decisions and stuck to them.

Thank you, Father, for everything I am learning from Vicky. Thank you; also, for bringing her to me, she gives me someone to fight for. She has brought a joy as well. It's remarkable to me that you sent her here, just when I needed your help the most. I know it's not over, but I thank you, for getting me this far.

Her praises seemed like the prayer before the battle, and she sensed that there was a battle coming up. She would be tested and would go through a trial, but it would show her a strength she didn't know she had.

But first she needed to be refreshed in her spirit.

Cara and Vicky got into the car, and drove to church.

The church was in a single story building that had once been a warehouse. It had been renovated into a comfortable place to worship.

When Cara and Vicky arrived, they arrived with a few other families. Cara looked at the families with young children, and there was one family with three kids who seemed to be about Vicky's age. As she watched them, she realized just how much Vicky had become like a temporary daughter to her. Just as Cara had become a temporary guardian to her.

When they stepped out of the car, Vicky asked, "Hey, will you skip with me?"

"What?" Cara replied.

"Skip. You know step-hop, step-hop, step-hop. Like this," Vicky demonstrated how to skip.

"Please, Cara? Will you please skip with me?"

Cara thought, *Why not?* so she told Vicky, yes, she would skip with her. They skipped together through the parking lot, and you know what, it was fun!

They stopped at the entrance and were greeted by Steve, who had been the official greeter for longer than Cara could remember.

"That was some nice skipping," he said with a warm smile on his face.

Cara started to blush, and Vicky said, "It was fun!"

"That's good," he said. "Welcome ladies. Cara, I've been praying for you, how have you been?"

"I've been uh...busy. Thank you for your prayers," she looked at Vicky, "they're definitely helping."

"You're welcome," he said warmly. "It was God who asked me to. He wants you, and he's not done with you yet."

Her heart leapt for joy, God was looking for her! She had known it, but it was way better to hear it.

"Thank you," she said.

She and Vicky walked into the building, and Vicky asked immediately, "Can I go to children's service?"

"Yes, you may. In fact, we can sign you up right now. The classrooms are just this way."

Cara led Vicky down a hallway toward the Sunday school rooms. Once they found the right classroom, Cara and Vicky walked in.

The room was similar to a kindergarten classroom; there were building blocks along one wall, a small toy kitchen, bins of toys, and a long table with small chairs around it.

Cara told the teacher, "This is Vicky; she's a cousin of mine who's visiting from another state. How do I sign her in?"

"Oh, you can just sign her in, here."

The teacher handed her a clipboard with a sign-in sheet on it.

"Do you need to know about food allergies?"

Vicky shot Cara a look that said, "What're you doing?"

Then the teacher answered and said, "We don't give out snacks, because there are too many allergies. That way we don't have to do any tailoring. It's a lot easier."

"Good," Cara remarked. *God, am I doing the right thing by leaving her here*, she prayed.

Yes, just go. With that, Cara filled out the sign-in sheet. Vicky was starting to play with the other children, "Bye, Vicky, see you after church."

"Bye Cara," she said.

"I think she'll be fine," the teacher told her.

Cara looked one last time, and then she walked toward the sanctuary. It felt strange to walk without Vicky, for she had only left her once before, and that was when she went to talk to her grandfather.

So she prayed, *God, I'm a little nervous about leaving Vicky, please protect her.* Taking a deep breath, she decided that she would trust God, and leave the outcomes to Him.

She walked into the sanctuary. Right away, she saw friends that she didn't realize she had missed, and they missed her. Then a new thought hit her: she had not come to church, because she was busy and hadn't wanted to. What she didn't realize, she had missed opportunities of fellowship and being able to grow spiritually. She had put her own desires ahead of fellowship.

In the sanctuary, Cara saw her friend Margie Callahan. Margie had been a friend since high school, and she was especially excited to see Cara. Cara and Margie were the kind of friends who could pick up almost where they left off, no matter how much time had passed. When they saw each other, they sat and began to talk.

As they talked, Cara realized that God was just such a friend. There would be times she would be further away from Him, but she could always come back to Him. All good relationships are from God to show us His love. The hard relationships are to teach us love, patience, endurance, forgiveness, and understanding.

Hard relationships teach us to love in that when you ask God to show you how He sees the person you're in conflict with, He will show you His love for them. Your view changes, and you no longer see with a view clouded by your own resentments, judgments, and/or hatreds; but you see them in love. God's love transforms lives.

Margie and Cara talked, and Cara was amazed how easy it was to reconnect. Unfortunately, they didn't have a lot of time to talk, because the worship team came onto the stage, and it was time for the service to start.

The worship team started with the song, "Blessed Be (Your Name)."

God, Cara prayed, *come and fill this place. Help me to worship You how you want to be worshipped.*

The next song, "The Solid Rock," was one that went straight to her heart. As the music played, she prayed that God would help her find her way. One question that kept coming up was: *God, what do you want me to do with my life?* Or she would put it as: *God, how do you want me to serve you? How do you want me to share your love?*

With Vicky, she heard Him say. *Share my love with her. As you share stories with her, as you tuck her in at night, as you wish her well before you go to bed, as you instruct and teach her the way she should go, you are influencing her for me, and that is how you share my love.*

Thank you, Father. For showing me these things, Cara said silently.

Cara, I love you because you exist. It's not because of what you've done, or where you've been. I AM your God, and you are my child.

Her breath caught, and her eyes became misty.

She felt a small burst of cool air go over her arms, and it wasn't from the air conditioning. She smiled.

God, please help me this week as I go back to work, Cara prayed. *Lead me, I pray. Don't let Ted or Ron get Vicky.*

Do not worry, I've got her. She is going to be alright.

Then the chain of worry ceased, and a peace reigned in her heart. *Thank you, Father God, for taking care of her and me.*

The pastor of the church came to the front in that moment.

"Thank you, worship team," he said, and then to the people seated before him he said, "Now would you stand and greet one another?"

Cara stood and gave a hug to Margie whom she was sitting next to, and shook the hands of others around her.

Then Pastor Mark asked the congregation to come back.

"If you remember last week we covered Acts 8:26-40. Philip teaches an Ethiopian God's word. This week, we'll discuss Saul's conversion on the way to Damascus.

"If you recall, according to Acts chapter 8:3, 'Saul made havoc of the church, entering every house, and dragging off men and women, committing them to prison.'

"The story in Acts 9 (you can follow along if you like in your Bibles)."

Several Bibles were flipped open to the book of Acts chapter 9.

"...Acts chapter nine starts out with Saul, 'still breathing threats and murder against the disciples of the Lord.' Oh, that's not a nice guy. What's more, he 'asked the high priest for letters from him to the synagogues of Damascus, so that if he found any who were of the Way, whether men or women, he might bring them bound to Jerusalem.'

"'As he journeyed he came near Damascus, and suddenly a light shone round about him from heaven.

"'Then he fell to the ground, and heard a voice saying to him, "Saul, Saul, why are you persecuting me?"

"'And he said, "Who are you, Lord?" The Lord said, "I am Jesus whom you are persecuting. It is hard for you kick against the goads."

"'So he, trembling and astonished, said, "Lord, what do you want me to do?" The Lord said to him, "Arise and go into the city, and you will be told what you must do."

"'The men who journeyed with him stood speechless, hearing a voice but seeing no one.

"'Then Saul arose from the ground, and when his eyes were opened he saw no one. But they led him by the hand and brought him into Damascus.

"'And he was three days without sight, and neither ate nor drank.'

"It's interesting, I think, that the song "Amazing Grace" also talks about being blind; one line in particular is, 'I once was blind, but now I see.' To be blind is to be in darkness. Jesus said, "I am the light of the world. Whoever follows me will never walk in darkness but have the light of life.

"Saul when he was throwing men and women into prison must've been in darkness. This, of course, is the same man who went on to say that he was content in all things whether bound or free. Saul was scholar in the Jewish law, but he didn't know who Jesus was until Jesus met him on the way to Damascus. The law did not save his life, that's not the job of the law. The law is only a tool to point to our need for a savior. What Paul wrote in the New Testament could not have been written, unless he had had a life change. He went from being a persecutor of the church to the father of the church. Jesus met him on the road, and took him from being in darkness to being in God's light.

"Friends, in other words, if when you don't know Jesus, you're in spiritual darkness, and then when you do, and commit your life to Jesus, it will be as if you see, and you will be in God's glorious light.

"I want to leave you with two thoughts; the first comes from Philippians 4:4-7: 'Rejoice in the Lord always. I will say it again: Rejoice! Let your gentleness be evident to all. The Lord is near. Do not be anxious about anything, but in everything, by prayer and petition, with thanksgiving, present your requests to God. And the peace of God which transcends all understanding will guard your hearts and your minds in Christ Jesus.'

"My second thought to leave you with is this: Jesus died and rose again in three days, and Saul was blind for three days."

"God still changes lives today. When I met my wife Kate, I didn't know the Lord, but she introduced me to Jesus. When I accepted Jesus into my heart, he changed me from the inside out. If you don't know Jesus, I welcome you to come up to one our deacons or myself, and just ask Jesus into your heart. Then I ask you to walk in that, and live out your faith. He will change your life.

"As we close, I want you to know that God did not leave Saul in that state, nor did he abandon him, but Saul later becomes Paul, the father of the church. God did not leave or abandon Saul, and he won't abandon you in what you're going through.

"Let's pray. Father God, I thank you for this opportunity to stand up here sharing your word. Thank you for changing my heart. For everyone who is here, I just ask that you come and meet them where they are. Father God, bless everyone here, with your love and your grace. Help them to know that you are good. Also, please help them to see you in an entirely different way. For the people who come up here, whether beginning a relationship with you the first time or rededicating their lives to you, make an impact in their lives. God, please direct them to you forever more. In Your Word it says, 'We did not choose you, but you chose us and appointed us to go bear fruit–fruit that will last.' Thank you Father God, for Your Word that we are able to read here today. In Jesus's name I pray, and everyone says..."

"Amen!" the entire congregation said.

"Amen," the pastor echoed. "Saul lived to share the Gospel of Jesus Christ; my prayer is that each of you walks in the same. God is at work here, and I hope you have a chance to see it. Those who believe Jesus died for their sins will get to have everlasting life. God's not done here, and he is still working in each of our lives. Now, go, be the church."

The doors leading to the foyer were opened. Cara felt God leading her to rededicate her life to Jesus, so she made her way to the front. She went up to meet the assistant pastor with Margie close behind. There, they prayed over her as they laid hands on her.

Cara started, "Oh, Father God, I need you. I know I've gotten far from you, please continue to restore my life, and please help me to never get this far away from you again. I know there are going to be hardships this week, give me strength and wisdom to go through it. God, I don't want to live without you, I can't live without you. Help me to carry forward this new feeling, I am feeling right now. As well, help me to do the right thing, no matter what is going on around me."

The assistant pastor continued, "I would also like to ask, that Cara would be a light to everyone in the situation. You would see her through, whatever it is. Whether it is relational, work-related, or even family. Bless her in this journey."

Lastly Margie added, "Thank you, Father God, for bringing my dear friend back to church. My heart is filled with warmth to hear that Cara desires to come back to you God. I thank you for answering my prayers."

Cara opened her eyes, *Margie has been praying for me? Margie wants me to have relationship with you, God, as much as I want to have relationship with you.*

Listen to what she has to say.

"...God, please help her to see just how much you love her. I also ask that she would know that you are God, and you are all that she needs. No matter where you will have her go, or what you will have her do (even if it's far from me), help her to lean on you, God. Even when it's hard, she would lean on you. In Jesus's name, I pray, amen."

"Amen," Cara and the assistant pastor echoed.

"Thank you, both of you," Cara said. "Margie, I didn't know you were praying for me. Thank you."

"Of course, I would. You're such a dear friend, that I hated seeing you so far from God. I'm not giving up on you, just as God did not give up on me. But you need to ask God to show you any sin in your life that you may repent, turning away from it. Because if sin stays open in your life, you will fall right back into it, and drift away from God again. Ask God to forgive you, that you may be set free from it."

"Thank you, again, Margie. I am so blessed to have you as a friend."

"Thank you. I am blessed to have *you* as a friend."

Cara gave Margie a quick embrace.

"I have to go pick up my cousin's daughter, she's waiting for me in Sunday school. We should get together sometime. I am busy right now, but I am hoping things smooth out soon. Call me."

"I will," Margie said.

"Please pray for me this week. I am entering some trials. I can't give you the details right now, but know that it's going to be bumpy up ahead for me."

"I will."

Cara left the sanctuary and headed for Vicky's classroom. There were parents there signing out their kids. As soon as Vicky saw Cara, she ran up to her throwing her arms around her.

"Cara!" she exclaimed. She shoved a coloring sheet into her hand. "I made this for you; it's a picture of the miracle of Jesus walking on the water. That's what we learned today. Turn it over, turn it over."

Cara flipped the sheet over; the words, "To: Kara, From: Vicky," were printed in orange crayon. Cara smiled, it was definitely from Vicky: the handwriting was lop-sided and was from a hand getting used to writing.

"Thank you," Cara replied. "I think this should go up on the fridge at home, what do you think?"

"I think so!"

"She did well," the teacher informed her, as Cara signed her name on the sign-out sheet.

"Good." Then to Vicky she asked, "Do you have everything? Are you ready to go?"

"Yep!"

They walked outside.

"Cara, I like your church, I had fun. Can I come back?"

"We'll see," Cara told her.

"So, did you know that Jesus walked on water?"

"I did."

"Did you know that God is so amazing?"

"I guess I did."

They walked to Cara's car. On the way back to Cara's apartment complex, they listened to the radio.

***

That night Cara was not able to sleep. Finally, she got out of bed and walked to the living room. Vicky was sleeping as a tree in the bedroom.

Cara sat down on the couch, reaching for her Bible on the coffee table.

"God," she whispered, "how did I get so far from you? How did I end up not reading my Bible or going to church? What is the sin in my life, which Margie was talking about?"

You're independence from me, she heard the quiet voice say.

What do you mean by, 'Independence from you'?

You sought independence more than me. It became a barrier between you and me. Independence is not a bad thing, when it's in its rightful place. When it is all you think about and all you seek, it becomes a worthless idol.

My desire for independence became an idol for me?

Yes, an idol, something that is worshipped instead of me.

Oh, God, I'm so sorry. Please help me to never put anything between you and me again. Help me to put you first.

After a pause, Cara asked, *God, am I right in keeping Vicky here?*

Look in your Bible.

Where?

Look in Exodus chapter 2.

Ok.

Cara turned on the lamp next to her, and opened her Bible to Exodus chapter 2. She began to read the first few verses.

"When she saw he was a beautiful child, she hid him three months." The passage was talking about Moses being hid from Pharaoh, when Pharaoh ordered the deaths of all Israelite males two years and younger.

Lord, do you mean me hiding Vicky from Ron and Ted?

Yes, that's what I mean. Vicky would have fallen into the hands of Ron and Ted, if I hadn't sent her to you. Moses lived to serve me and you are serving me by saving her.

What about tomorrow? What shall I do then?

Don't worry. I've got her and you.

She sat quietly for a moment.

Then it occurred to her that sin was a cancer of the soul. Small and almost invisible, at first, but as time goes by it only grows. Sometimes, it will cut off circulation to the area it starts in. Parts can break off and spread to other areas, where it continues to grow. Cancer leads to death, if left on its own; just like sin. "The wage of sin is death, but the gift of God is eternal life in Christ Jesus our Lord." (Romans 6:23)

That's why Jesus's sacrifice is so important: without it we could not have a relationship with God. The moment when we believe Jesus Christ died for our sins, is when we are saved.

Thank you, God, Cara said silently.

She went to the kitchen, grabbed a cup, and started to fill it with tap water.

Sin is a thief, isn't it? she asked taking a drink.

Sin is a thief, and the thing it steals the most is time.

Time?

Yes, time.

She reflected upon that. When someone has sin, they lose that time to guilt, shame, and/or fear. Time spent in sin is lost and cannot be gained back, even just a moment. Sin also can burn bridges, separate families, or make an individual hard to trust. *Life is too short to miss out on even a moment of what God has for me or my life,* Cara thought.

God, thank you for not giving up on me. Or Vicky.

With that she headed back to bed.

6

THE BIG DAY

Monday came early and quickly. Cara prodded Vicky gently awake.

"Cara, what's wrong?" she asked, rubbing the sleep out of her eye.

"Nothing is wrong," Cara assured her, "I'm going into work today, and I need you to go to a neighbor's home."

"Who?"

"Her name is Lavender, and she lives right across the way from me."

"OK," she said.

"She will keep you safe."

"OK," she said again.

Cara started to grab things for work. She pulled Vicky's picture off the fridge, "Can I bring this into work with me?"

"Sure."

Cara patted herself down, "I have my cell phone, my keys, the picture, am I missing anything?" she asked herself.

"Do you have shoes?" Vicky asked.

She looked down at her feet, "I need shoes," she said walking to her bedroom.

She grabbed a pair and put them on. Then she walked Vicky over to Lavender's apartment across the way.

On the drive to work, she turned off the radio, and she said aloud, "God, I need you with every part of my being, in all aspects of my life; from the deepest parts of my heart that craves your presence to the shallowest places that want material things. I can't live without you, and I never want to. God, without you, anything I try to do will not have eternal value. Every day, every moment, every thought I need you. Thank you for not giving up on me." With that she felt a peace wash over her.

She arrived at work on time to catch her breath. When the work day started, she was tense and on edge. She was aware of everything at once: clicks of mice, tapping of keys, people talking on phones, ringing of phones, pencils being sharpened; it was a cacophony of noises. She kept special tabs on her supervisor, Mr. Anderson.

He stayed in his office most of the morning; sometimes he was on the phone. She was looking for any indication that he knew she had Vicky.

Cara got up to get water, at one point.

When she got back to her workstation, she tried to do some work.

Here's what it sounded like:

Click-click-click-click-click-Ding-"Ah!"

Click-click-click-Ding-"Oh!"

Click-click-Ding-Ding-Ding-"No!"-"Err..."

Every time she made an error, the computer would ding at her. She had been trained not to make a sound. It seemed she had drawn quite a lot of attention. A woman who worked in the next workstation asked, "Cara, are you alright?"

She was about to answer family issues, when she heard, "Why are you making so many mistakes?"

She jumped in fear and surprise. Behind her stood her boss, Mr. Dean Anderson leaning on the walls of the cubicle, glaring down at her. She noticed everyone who had been standing, slowly sink back into their cubicles, so they wouldn't be caught watching her.

"Cara, I said why are you making all those mistakes?"

"I'm sorry, sir," she said, "I have a lot of things on my mind."

He replied, "If it happens again, I'll have to fire you."

"Indeed," she said.

He walked back to his office, people got back to work, and she sat there a moment.

She was half-tempted to pick up the phone and call her neighbor to check in on Vicky. Her hand hovered over the receiver, but then she thought, *No, if there is a problem I would have heard something.*

Pray for them, she heard in her mind.

She started to pray, *Protect them, Father. Please don't let them find out Vicky is there.*

Too late.

Oh no. Please give Lavender wisdom. Should I go?

No, stay for the moment. They don't have Vicky.

Right about that time, Ron and Ted walked in. Her heart jumped several beats in her chest. Upon seeing them, Mr. Anderson ushered them quickly into his office. They almost had hops in their steps. Without thinking, she grabbed a stack of papers, and started feeding them into the copier. She tried to catch as much of their conversation as she possibly could. She heard words like; girl, plant, flower, and wild flower.

She opened the hatch to the copier, and laid a sheet on the glass. In her haste, she hit the start button. It whirred and made a single copy.

"Excuse me, can I make some copies?" a coworker asked.

"Uh, sure."

Right at that moment, Mr. Anderson's door opened and Ron and Ted came out. She felt embarrassed that she had been caught. She grabbed the copies she had made, and the sheets she had fed into it. It wasn't until she had gotten back to her workstation, that she realized she had forgotten the sheet on the glass.

From her cubicle, she watched as the coworker lifted the lid. He handed the sheet to Ron. Ron examined it, and handed it to Ted. Both of them became visibly more excited. She looked down at the pile of copies. Right on top of the pile, was a copy made of Vicky's picture.

"Oh no," she gasped.

What do I do? she prayed silently.

She looked up and saw them heading toward the elevator. Her heart rate increased drastically.

God, what have I done? she asked as she started to run after them. They made it to the elevator, before she could reach them. It was not about her, it was about protecting Vicky, and that gave her the energy she needed to run.

She ran down the stairs to the ground floor. When she got to the lobby, they were already racing outside. Even with adrenaline, they had enough of a head start, that they would make it to one of their cars before she could get to them. She did the most logical thing she could think of, she ran toward the parking garage across the street to get *her* car. She got in the elevator, and punched the button for the third floor. On the short ride up, she started to breathe.

Oh, God, please don't let them get to her.

The elevator pulled up to the third level. Before the doors were fully opened, she burst through. She was running at top speed. Thankfully, her car wasn't too far from the elevator. She pushed the unlock button on the remote. She opened the door, and got in.

She started her car, and sped down the garage spiral to the toll booth. Two cars were ahead of her. She waited for them to pay. When it was her turn, she pointed to her monthly pass, and they let her through.

Then she was speeding on the one-way roads. She came to a red light, and had to wait for a commuter train to pass.

God, she prayed, *please don't let them reach Vicky.*

Already done.

Cara kept driving. The urgency died some. Jaywalkers crossed the street in front of her.

Throughout the drive, she didn't see any sign of Ron or Ted's car.

When she arrived at her apartment complex, there was a police car and a news van.

Her heart dropped, *What happened?*

There has been a break-in.

She pulled her car over to the side of the road, and parked. She walked up to a reporter.

"What happened?" she demanded of the reporter. The camera man was getting ready to move out.

"There's been a home invasion," he said to her.

He began to walk away.

"I live here," she insisted.

He stopped and looked at her, "The men responsible broke in about fifteen minutes ago."

After a moment he asked, "You wouldn't be the tenant in 5A, would you?"

"Cara Stenfeld, yes, that's me."

"Well, two men entered your apartment fifteen minutes ago."

She thought back fifteen minutes; she had been on the road heading home. Then she thought about Ron and Ted coming into the building excited. They must have known. How did they know? When did they find out? What she didn't know was that they had begun watching her after she saw them at the Rhododendron Garden, and while Vicky and Cara traveled to Washington to visit Vicky's grandpa, they watched Cara's apartment. When she didn't come back, they decided to try another day. Sunday, they drove by Cara's apartment, right as she was listening to the worship band at church. Had she been home, they would have gotten Vicky.

"Miss, are you okay?" the reporter asked Cara.

"I...I need some time to think." She sat on a boulder nearby.

"How did this happen?"

"What we figure is that someone kicked in the door. A neighbor called 911 fifteen minutes ago saying she heard a bang, 'like someone kicked in a door.' "

Her adrenaline rush was starting to end. She became jittery and tired. The emotions and the high-stress of the day left her, and she wanted to cry. An officer walked over to where she was sitting.

"Are you Cara Stenfeld?" he asked.

"Yes," she said.

He glanced at the reporter, "I'm sure he told you that your apartment has been broken into. Is there somewhere we can talk privately?"

"There is a park just up the road from here," she told him.

"That'll do just fine."

They walked to the park, about a third of a mile away. Then when it was safe to talk, he turned to her.

"Do you know who could've done this?" he asked.

"I know exactly who did this."

"You do?" he pulled out a small notepad and pencil.

"Yep, they're coworkers of mine. They're names are Ron Gipp and Ted Zywick. They were looking for a..."

"A what?" the officer prompted.

God, I need help.

The truth, she heard in her mind.

"So, what were those men looking for in your apartment?" he asked.

Cara took a big breath to steady her nerves, "A little girl."

"How old is the little girl, if you don't mind my asking?"

"She's five."

"OK," he said beginning to process what she had just said. "Is she, by chance, a Potted person?"

"Yeah." She was caught off guard by the question.

"I thought so. We found some soil on the floor."

"Oh," she replied. "Th..."

"What do you mean by 'Oh'?"

"The plant that Ron and Ted got from my apartment was, in fact, just an indoor plant."

"So where's the real little girl?"

"She's with a neighbor."

"How did you end up with a young Potted person?"

"Her family was on a road trip, and they stopped at the gas station near my apartment complex. Vicky and her mom went into the store, and the two men — my coworkers — showed up. Vicky hid and her mom left. The family drove off. Vicky walked across the street to my apartment complex."

"So the men separated her from her parents, and she just happened to go to your door, a single woman who happens to know and work with the men who separated her." He shook his head, "The odds are low for this to happen like this."

Then she replied, "You have to have a little faith. Unless God had been involved, this would not have happened. The funny thing is I was getting ready for work, when she came to my door."

"Can you prove that you weren't at the scene when she was separated from her parents?"

"I live on the top floor of an apartment complex. The stairs leading up to my apartment echo considerably. If I were to leave, someone was bound to have heard me. Vicky came to me at five till six in the morning, and then she and I left not too long after. She crossed a two-lane road, and she crossed in front of the complex to get to my apartment."

"Alright, I'll talk to the neighbors." Then the officer said, "I'm not saying this will ever happen again, but if it does, you do need to call the authorities. They will know what to do. Do not take it into your own hands, even if you fear for the child's safety. Do you understand?"

"What about cops who would try to use her for her abilities?"

"The majority of us are good, hard-working citizens just trying to pay our bills and keep crime down."

"OK."

They started to swing back toward the apartment complex. When they neared her apartment complex, he pulled out a business card, "Here," he said handing it to her, "is my card, if you see those men, don't be afraid to call me."

He pointed to the number on the card, "That number will take you directly to the police station."

"Thank you," she said putting the card in her purse.

"Do you want me to walk you to your apartment?"

"No, I think I can manage," she said.

"OK."

She walked around the corner, and down the sidewalk. At the bottom of the stairs, she paused a moment, as she prepared herself for what was at the top of the stairs. Then she ran up the stairs, and stepped into her apartment. The front door was wide open, and hanging by a corner. The apartment was in shambles, it looked like a wild animal trampled through the apartment. Stuff was strewn everywhere. Her apartment had been kept neat and in order, but you couldn't tell by looking at it.

Then emotions stirred inside of her, she was angry and she felt violated. In that moment, she determined that she would no longer work for a man who would hire men to do this. Just a few days prior, she had decided she wanted to leave, but she was afraid of looking for employment elsewhere. Now to see the difference between where she had been and this new change growing in her was incredible.

Then she remembered Vicky. She was still at Lavender's. Cara walked over and knocked.

Lavender opened the door a crack, and before Cara could speak she said, "Cara, we've been waiting for you."

"You have? I came as soon as I could."

"Yes, she's quite shaken up."

Lavender opened the door all the way, "You should carry her back to your apartment."

Carry her, Cara wondered as she walked in.

In the middle of the dining room was a black flower pot with a bush of flowers in it.

Unlike most dining rooms, Lavender did not have a table; instead she had empty floor space.

"I tried to tell her it was ok to turn back, but she insisted she would not turn back until you came and told her it would be ok," Lavender explained to her.

"How did you know she turned into a plant?" she asked.

She turned to face her, and she lowered her sunglasses to wink at her. Her eyes were a vivid shade of light blue.

Cara had been in the right proximity for Vicky to run to her apartment. One more blessing: Lavender, the neighbor across the way, was an older Potted person.

"I know these things," she told Cara as she put her sunglasses back into place.

She carefully picked up Vicky's pot, "Will you make sure the door is open for me?"

"Yes."

Vicky was heavy, but no different than any other plant her size. Cara carried her with care across to her apartment. She set her down on the floor of her apartment. Lavender retreated back to her apartment, and closed the door.

Cara placed her door over the door frame, as much as she could. Then she crouched down, "Vicky," she said gently, "it's me, it's Cara."

Nothing happened.

She tried again, "Vicky, you're safe now, and it's ok to turn back."

Still nothing happened, not even a movement of leaves.

This time, she tried a different tactic, "Vicky, please turn back, I want to see you."

With that, branches started to straighten out, and as they did, they also became thicker. Then they began to stick together like play-doh. The branches formed her shape, then she was back to being a little girl again, and all the leaves and flowers were gone. As soon as she was a little girl, she threw her arms around Cara's shoulders and wept.

"Cara," she said when she could speak, "the bad guys got away."

"I know."

"If they got away, won't they try to get me again? I mean, are they going to hurt me?"

"Not if I have anything to say about it."

God, please help me, she prayed.

I am, He replied.

She sought God's help for the rest of the day. She prayed for wisdom, and she asked God to continuously protect Vicky.

7

A BIG STRENGTH

The next day, Cara went to work to clear her personal belongings from her workstation. Mid-way through, her boss Mr. Anderson came to her and her workstation.

Get angry, but do not sin, she heard in her mind.

Then her boss said, "Ah good, Cara, I want to see you in my office right away."

It's okay to get angry, but do not sin.

"Okay," she said. She set the picture frame in the box she had brought.

She walked into Mr. Anderson's office a little nervously.

"Close the door," he told her.

She closed the door, and sat down in the chair facing his desk. She tucked her hair behind her ears.

He took a seat behind his big desk, his fingers interlacing together on his desk.

"I'll get right to it," he said. "You have something that I want."

"What do I have that you want?"

"You have a little girl about five or six."

She was silent, so he opened a drawer and pulled out Vicky's coloring page.

"I want her," he said throwing the sheet of paper toward her, "and I'm willing to pay you an extra three dollars an hour, plus a one thousand dollar bonus."

She looked at the picture Vicky drew for her, *Jesus walked on the water*, the caption read.

The verse "I can do all things through Christ who gives me strength," came to her mind. She remembered the promise she had made at the Rhododendron Garden, "*I will protect you no matter what.*"

So she firmly told her boss, "No."

"Excuse me?"

"I said 'no'. You want me to compromise the moral integrity of a little girl?" she felt sick inside.

She rose to leave.

"Cara, they're plants."

"Yes, but they're people too. If turning in a little girl is the only way to get the promotion I have been passed up for ever since I started working here; then, I quit. Nothing is worth that. I'm not going to work in a place like that."

With that, she left his office, and dashed to her desk. She felt strong and bold, in a way she hadn't in a long time.

She also felt like she had to hurry to get out of there. As she walked past Mr. Anderson on the way out, he said, "So, you quit just like that?"

"Yep."

When she reached the lobby, she handed her employee badge to the receptionist. Then she left.

She half jogged across the street to the parking garage. She was excited and practically walking on air. Her boss had been a strong force of wind that had been pressing her down, but now she stood her ground. She had almost forgotten about the rain, and it was about to rain on her parade.

She pressed the button on the remote, and got in on the driver's side, and set the box on the passenger's side.

She turned on the ignition and Ron and Ted jumped into the backseats. Immediately, she threw the gearshift into reverse and gunned it into a cement post directly behind her. Then it was like she was watching a slow motion video, she was aware of every shard of glass from the back window. Just as suddenly everything stopped. She looked at the dazed men in the backseat. One was bleeding, and the other seemed to be unconscious.

She unbuckled her seatbelt, and hopped out of the car.

"I'm sorry!" she cried. Right as she did, a parking attendant was coming up to see what had happened.

"Call 911!" she insisted.

"Ma'am, are you okay?" he asked her.

"I am...fine. Call 911, I rammed my car into the post."

"I heard. Ma'am, I think you need to sit down."

A crowd was starting to gather to watch the spectacle.

"The two men jumped into my car, and I drove back. They were trying to hurt me."

"I'll check it out."

Cara stood by while the parking attendant looked inside her car.

Out of the corner of her eye, Cara saw a man on his cell phone.

"There's been an accident at the 10th and Morrison parking garage in downtown Portland," she heard him say. "Third floor. Yeah, there's a woman here." Then he asked Cara, "Are you all right to talk?"

"Yeah," she said.

He handed Cara the receiver.

"Hello?" she said.

"Hello, this is Andrea with 911; can I have your name please?"

"Cara Stenfeld."

"OK, Ms. Stenfeld, I hear there's been an accident. Can you give me the details?"

"Uh, sure. Two men broke into my apartment yesterday, and they jumped into my car, today. Their names are Ron Gipp and Ted Zywick."

"Are there any serious injuries?"

"Well, a parking attendant went to take a look."

"I'm sending Portland Police and paramedics. Do you mind staying on the line with me?"

She looked at the man who owned the phone, "Is it okay to stay on the line?" she asked.

"Stay on, as long as you need," he told her.

"OK," she told the 911 operator.

Just then, the parking attendant who went to check out the damage came up to her.

He said, "I'm sorry, your car has been totaled."

"What about the men?" Cara asked.

"They are unconscious."

"Oh no," she said.

"What?" Andrea asked gently.

"The men in my car are unconscious, and the parking attendant says my car has been totaled."

"The paramedics should be arriving there any minute."

"OK." At that moment, the sirens were heard coming their way, and within moments police officers and emergency vehicles were coming up the parking garage.

"They're here," Cara informed her.

"OK, they can take over from here. I'm going to hang up now."

"OK." She hung up, and handed the phone back to its owner. An officer came up to her.

"What happened?" he asked her.

"I was starting my car, when two men jumped into my car, so I crashed it into a pole, they were in back, and they weren't buckled."

"Are they still in the car?" he asked.

"Yes," the parking attendant reported. "I checked on them, they are both unconscious."

The officer signaled the fire and rescue truck, "Alright," he said. "We'll go up there," then he looked at Cara, "as for you, ma'am you need to stay where you are."

"Yes sir," she complied.

Five minutes later, an ambulance arrived. Twenty minutes after that, the ambulance was driving toward the exit.

The officer approached Cara again.

"They'll be okay," he told her. "Neither one of them will be able to move around a lot. Their injuries are pretty serious, but they'll survive. They are being transported to the hospital by ambulance. Once they're stable, they will be sent to jail, where they will not bother you anymore."

"Thank you," she said.

"Would you like me to call someone for you?"

"Yes, will you please call a friend of mine?"

She gave him Margie's cell phone number, then he handed her the phone.

It rang for a bit, and then she heard, "Hello?"

"Hi, Margie, it's Cara," she said.

"This is a strange number. Where are you calling from?"

"A police officer's. Anyways, my car is going to have to be towed."

"Towed? What happened?"

"I was in an accident, so would you mind taking me home?"

"Yeah, where are you?"

"I'm in a parking garage across from my work."

"OK."

"Thank you, Margie."

"I'll be there in ten-ish minutes."

"Bye."

They hung up, and she handed the phone to the officer.

"Thank you."

"Will you be alright?" he asked her.

"Yeah, I'll be fine."

"Don't worry about your car, I'll call a tow truck to tow your car away," an attendant told her.

Margie arrived, "You look awful," she told her as she got into her car.

***

On the way to Cara's apartment, she told her what had happened. Margie dropped her off at her apartment.

Later that day, Cara heard a knock at her front door. Looking through the peephole, she saw a man and a woman standing there. *Could it be?* she thought. She opened the door a crack.

"Are you Cara Stenfeld?" the man demanded of her, he was tall with dark, graying hair, broad shoulders, and brown eyes like a tree in golden evening light.

The woman with him was also tall, but she was thin with frizzy, red hair and green eyes like grass in the spring.

"My name is Douglas Fields," the man said, Cara heard movement behind her, "and this is my wife Lily, and we're...we're..."

Cara felt a tug on her shirt; she put a finger for one moment. She closed the door for a bit.

"What is it?!"

"Open the door," Vicky told her.

Cara did so, and Vicky raced outside to throw her arms around them.

"Mom, Daddy!" she exclaimed.

Douglas Fields lifted her up, and put her on his shoulder. He held her there as he said, "Victoria, Victoria. My precious, sweet Victorious Princess, Victoria. How I've missed you!"

When Cara first saw the man, he looked strong, but he melted as he held his little girl. Cara saw in that moment how strong love can be. Her heart melted with them, and suddenly she wanted to call her dad to tell him how much she loved him. She also thought about her Heavenly Father, how he held her the entire week that Vicky was with her. Then she thought, *God holds all of His children.*

Lily Fields explained, "I'm sorry we couldn't get here sooner, the two men were watching the area around the gas station, closely. If we came and got Vicky before they were gone, the safety of our older children might have been jeopardized. So we laid low in a hotel room nearby, until we could safely retrieve our daughter. I'm sorry it took so long."

Cara responded, "It was okay, she really wasn't a problem. It was…nice."

Douglas said to Vicky, "Vicky, I'm going to hand you over to your mom."

"Why?" Vicky asked.

"I want to talk to Miss Cara, for a moment."

"Oh, okay," she replied.

He handed her over to her mother, and then he said to Cara, "Cara, I know you lost a lot this week as you protected our daughter, but if there's anything you want, anything at all, all you have to do is ask."

"I would only like two things," she told him, "the first is a new job."

"That's doable," he said. "What's the other thing?"

She looked at Vicky, "I would like to see her grow up."

Vicky's parents exchanged a glance, "We can do that," Lily said slowly, "but it's not always safe for us to travel."

Then she asked Vicky, "Would you like to see Miss Cara, again?"

Vicky nodded her head profusely, "Yes!" she exclaimed.

"Alright."

Then Douglas said to Cara, "We are so grateful for what you've done for us, we simply cannot thank you enough."

"You're welcome," she replied. "It was kind of fun. It made me excited to have kids of my own, someday."

"Thank you, again," he said. Then he said, "We really should be heading home, Vicky, give Cara a hug."

Lily set Vicky on the ground, and Vicky embraced her, "Thank you, Cara Stenfeld!" Then she whispered, "Perhaps you'll come to our house."

"Time to go, Vicky," Lily told her.

"Perhaps, I will next month," Cara whispered back.

Douglas pulled out a bill fold and handed her a business card. "We'll be in touch," he told her.

Cara nodded her head, which was starting to hurt, "Indeed," she said.

"Bye," Cara said.

"Bye!" Vicky echoed.

"Bye," she repeated.

"Bye," Vicky said again. "See you next month! Bye!"

She and her parents walked down the stairs to their minivan waiting down below, and then they left. Cara walked into her apartment. She felt certain that one chapter in her life had ended, which meant it was time for the next chapter to begin, who knew what that would entail? The prospect of a fresh start was exciting and a little overwhelming. Her life was before her, and her old life was behind her. Beyond everything, she knew that no matter what lied ahead of her; God would be there to lead her through.

EPILOGUE

18 months later…

There was a knock on the door. Someone opened the door, and standing there was a ten-year-old girl. She had brown hair that reached just below her shoulders. In her hands was a small, silver pail with daisies in it.

"My parents asked me to give this to Cara."

Cara saw the reflection of the girl in the mirror.

"Thank you, Sarah. Why don't you put them on the table?"

She pointed to a small table near her. Sarah Fields made her way through the room from the door to the table Cara indicated. There were a lot of women in the room, but even so, Sarah moved through slowly and carefully. She was not comfortable among so many other people, but she maintained her composure. Normally Cara would have given Vicky's older sister a hug, but Cara was trying to not move. Cara's hair was in the clamping jaws of a curling iron that her sister-in-law was holding.

She told Sarah thank you. When the pot was set down, Sarah left the room quickly.

There was a note in the flowers, "To: Cara, With Love: The Fields Family." She knew the flowers were from the Fields family, but more importantly, she knew *who* the flowers were. Vicky Fields had been planning to be in the wedding ceremony, but she wanted to be the flowers, "That everybody would see."

A bouquet was challenging, because of Vicky's age (now seven), but a bouquet in a small container on the stage where Cara and her fiancée were to take their vows would be seen and could be bigger.

You could feel the excitement in the room. Ladies were talking, putting make-up on, and helping Cara get ready. More than anyone, Cara was excited. She had met her fiancée at a job interview. She had arrived ten minutes early, and had some time to sit. As she was sitting, a guy came in, and they started talking. Then she went in for the interview, but when she came back out he was gone. She didn't find out until after she was hired that the man she had seen in the lobby had been the interviewer's nephew, who came in frequently to visit, he had to leave early because an important call came in.

Cara and David started dating not too long after that. One date turned into two, which became three, which quickly led to four, five, and six. Until, they became fiancées.

Cara was absolutely amazed how God orchestrated everything: from her losing her job, to Vicky coming to her door, and even meeting David. Because she had saved Vicky's life, Vicky's dad used his connections in Portland to see who was hiring. Using Douglas's Portland connections, she was able to apply and be called in for an interview. When she showed up for the interview she met David who would later become her fiancée. David was the interviewer's nephew, and he was there that day to visit his uncle. There was an instant connection between them. She got the job, and she and David started dating not too long after that.

What Cara didn't realize, when she surrendered to God's will, He would lead her to the steps that would bring her back to him, and into a wonderful new life.

She felt like a child at Christmas who is getting exactly what they wanted, but they have to wait until Christmas to open their presents.

Of course, there were still last-minute details to attend to: Cara and her bridesmaids had to finish getting ready, the photos still had to be taken, and the chairs had to be set up.

Cara wondered every once in a while what her fiancée was doing to get ready. She imagined it was much simpler than everything it took for her to get ready. Her hair had to be done, her make-up had to be applied, and her nails had to be painted. Then she had to get into her dress, put her jewelry on, and her veil. Then after that, she would go down the aisle to become her fiancée's wife.

Mrs. David Matthews, she liked the sound of it. Every time she thought about him, her heart danced in her chest.

She loved him, that was for sure, and she was excited to begin her life with him.

As she walked down the aisle, one verse came to mind, "As for me and my house, we will serve the Lord."

As we close, reader, I want to ask you: where is your heart? Where is your hope? Are you stuck like Cara was, or are you free? Where do you put your trust? Where does your eternity lie? God is worth knowing, and He loves you just the way you are. Don't let an opportunity to have eternal life pass you by. Jesus died for the sins of all. All you have to do is believe that and receive Jesus as your savior. "Repent, then, and turn to God, that your sins may be blotted out, that times of refreshing may come from the Lord." (Acts 3:19)

The kingdom of Heaven is near.

AUTHOR'S NOTE

At seventeen, I was diagnosed with Aspergers Syndrome*. It was hard when I first got the diagnosis, because my first thought was that it was just one more thing to make me different. The truth is that this is how God made be to be. I am different, and I always have been. Now, there's a name to it, but the greatest thing I can be is who God created me to be.

In writing Vicky: The Flower Girl, I am sharing the passion God has given me for Him and for writing, and I am sharing Jesus in a unique way. I was once lost, but now I am found. My identity is Christ Jesus, and on no other ground shall I stand, for it is all sinking sand.

I am telling you this, so that you may understand why sometimes lines in the story may not make sense. For me, it's a challenge to try to think like someone who isn't on the autistic spectrum, because I don't think that way. One thing I've learned: it's okay to be different. He didn't make me to run with the crowds, just another in a sea of faces. He made me to stand out and be a light in this world as I share God's love through Jesus. Everyone is made to shine in God's glory.

God is using me because of my disability. When we are weak, He is strong. Our weaknesses exemplify our need for God. I want to be used by God, and I get excited at the prospect of sharing what He has done in my life.

God is my victory. Without Him, I can't do anything that will have eternal value. God saved my life, so how cool is it that I get to pass that on? Why wouldn't I share what God has done for me?

*Aspergers Syndrome is a communicative disorder on the autistic spectrum that affects a person's day-to-day activities in socialization, working, etc. The determination of how high functioning someone is determines where they are on autistic spectrum. Aspergers is usually considered a high functioning version of autism. There are all different levels and capabilities. Children, who have autism, may not look you in the eyes, when you try to speak to them, but they are very intelligent. In that way, being on the autistic spectrum presents a difference of abilities.

CPSIA information can be obtained
at www.ICGtesting.com
Printed in the USA
FSOW02n0727210515
7308FS